HER LAST BREATH

THE WATCHER
BOOK 1

STACY CLAFLIN

1

The Watcher

Hiding in safety

Everything is coming together perfectly. Couldn't have hoped for better. All the pieces are falling into place, and soon she'll be mine.

This has been my dream for so long. Didn't think it would ever happen. Might not have, organically. But I *made* it happen.

I did this. As soon as she realizes that, she'll know how much she means to me. What lengths I'll go to for her.

There's no limit to what I would do for my flower.

Nothing.

My breath hitches as the fancy car pulls up to the driveway. I'm too far away to see the driver.

Is that her?

The engine cuts, the lights go off, then the door flings open.

Anticipation makes me salivate, but I'll wait. I have to. There's no other choice. I've put too much into this to risk losing her over a snap decision, a lapse in judgment.

She steps out of the sedan—long bare legs flanked by high-heeled pumps and a shortish black skirt grab my attention. I squint, hold my hand over my eyes to focus.

The tension is too much.

It isn't her.

Disappointment runs through me. I'm tempted to break something but can't risk looking away for even a moment. Need to find out who *this* woman is and why she's in the driveway.

This is wrong, all wrong.

High Heels Lady flips back her long, straight, dark brown hair. Everything about this woman is wrong.

Because she isn't *her*.

Part of me wants to run up to her and shake her, demand answers.

I will remain patient. There has to be a reason for this madness. For this change in plans.

It could be any number of things. The scenarios are endless.

That's why I must hold myself together. I've come too far to let something so trivial get in my way.

This better be trivial.

I can't deal with a hitch. There's too much riding on this. I've been waiting so long already. Gone to all the effort of orchestrating this. No way will I let some random woman ruin everything.

My hands shake as the brown-haired woman sashays across the driveway as if she owns the place.

She doesn't. Not even close. Who is she, and why is she there?

This is all wrong. Anger roils through me in waves.

I take several deep breaths. I'm nothing if not patient, adaptable. Whatever this is, I can handle it.

One way or another. I'm ready for anything.

The sheathed knife in my pocket pokes me and reminds me of that much. I have options, even if some aren't ideal.

I'll give this situation a moment before I decide what to do. Something must be done.

Because this woman is not *her*.

That's a very big problem. For all three of us.

Every muscle in my body tenses as I watch her. Could she walk any slower? It's like she's trying to turn it into an Olympic sport.

Hurry up, already!

I take a deep breath. Can't afford to lose my patience. My temper will be next, and nobody wants that. Least of all me.

The woman pulls something from her bag.

What is it? I lean forward for a better look, but I'm too far away.

If I'd known everything would go off the rails like this, I'd have brought binoculars. Too late for that now.

Whatever it is, it's rectangular and long.

Odd. Now I'm curious. What is she doing on my flower's property, and what is she doing with that thing?

The woman steps in front of the For Sale sign.

I can't see what's she's doing.

Annoyance and curiosity battle within me. This might not be so bad, whatever the woman is doing.

She steps away.

Now it all makes sense.

There's a bold Sold banner across the sign.

She's letting everyone know the house is no longer available.

Because my flower, the love of my life is moving in—the person I fell in love with so many years ago. *She's* the one who's going to move in.

After all the effort I've expended to bring her here, she's finally going to be *mine*.

She just doesn't know it yet.

2

Fleur

Saturday, early evening

The sun is only starting to set as I turn down the road in the cute little suburban neighborhood. The houses are adorable, as to be expected. And they're all at least five times as big as the New York condo I left behind.

Good riddance.

Tears sting my eyes, but I ignore them. I'm not sad about walking away. I'm better off, and glad to have him across the country from me. No chance of accidentally running into him now. He wouldn't know what to do here in Washington state where I grew up.

I can't believe I'm back. It wasn't supposed to be this way. But here I am.

At least I'm on the other end of town from where my family lived.

From where she disappeared.

I shove that thought away as quickly as it came. A lump forms in my throat anyway.

Why did I return? There's too much heartache in this place.

That was why I fled as soon as I graduated. Not that it stopped bad things from happening here. The only times I've returned was to attend the funerals.

Maybe I should've moved somewhere else. Somewhere new. But I left so fast, and all I could think about was getting away from Ian and his unending supply of lies. If I had a dollar for every grand promise he'd failed to follow through on, I could buy an entire high rise apartment building.

Instead, I'm left with a minivan filled with every one of my earthly belongings. I bought it for the road trip home because it's big enough to hold all of my things and the mechanic said it would be reliable enough to get me from the east coast to the west coast.

And here I am, in one piece with all of my things. Everything Ian and I bought together is still with him. He wouldn't let me take even one thing we purchased together.

Typical.

Like I said, good riddance. I only wish I'd seen through his charm sooner.

Can't change the past—only the future. And mine is bright. If thirty really is the new twenty, then I'm golden. I have plenty of time to find someone who actually wants to settle down and have a family. Somebody who won't spew lies just because he thinks that's what I want to hear.

Ugh. I'm starting over, and here I am thinking about Ian. What's wrong with me?

New life, new start, new house.

The navigation system pulls me from my thoughts to let me know I've arrived at my destination.

I look left. My new house, bought sight unseen.

Clinging to the steering wheel with a death grip, I flip on my blinker then turn into the driveway.

The house *looks* like it's been sitting there for two years—because it has. Moss grows in parts of the roof, the grass is easily up to my knees, and the exterior could use a good scrubbing.

Fun.

But it's mine. I can use all the money I saved on the purchase to get everything fixed and still have plenty to spare for fun. Between my recent inheritance and my job—which easily traveled across the country with me—I won't have money worries for a long time.

That was one of the reasons I let Mia, my childhood best friend, talk me into buying this house. How could I turn down a fully furnished *house* at half the market value?

I couldn't.

Thankfully, I'm not superstitious like most other people—as evidenced by how long this adorable house has been for sale with the price sliding steadily over the last year.

I'm not most people.

No way would I let a little tainted history get in the way of my dreams.

Otherwise, I'd have been too scared to move into a murder house.

3

Fleur

Saturday, early evening

I cut the engine and turn to the passenger seat. "Zorro, wake up."

When the pup doesn't stir, I rub his ears until he does. One eye opens followed by the other. He lifts an ear and gives me a quizzical expression. The black spot around his right eye makes it even more adorable.

"We're home, little buddy."

He doesn't appear to believe me. Not that I blame him. We've been on the road forever.

He lifts his head as I open my door and nod toward the house. "You ready?"

Zorro yawns.

"You might change your mind when you see the yard."

When he doesn't budge, I get out and stretch. Still no movement, so I grab my purse then dig around for the house keys. Mia sent them to me before I started my road trip. There are definitely some perks to having a real estate agent as a best friend.

She sent me the complete set, save one that I asked her to hold onto. Hopefully I can keep my curiosity at bay and not beg her for that one. It's already giving me that itchy feeling.

Now isn't the time for that. I have other things to deal with first.

I study the façade of my new home. Nobody else would've mentioned this house to me. She said only a few people have even toured the house over the course of the last two years as it languished—and those were just looky-loos. Nobody serious.

I checked out the online listing, not expecting much, but could hardly believe my eyes. Ignoring the fact that someone died a bloody death in there, the house was amazing. Fully furnished because the previous residents obviously didn't take anything with them—one is dead and the other missing, and the bank who overtook the loan didn't pay to clean it out or even maintain it—it's the perfect place for me.

The woman who lived and died here had impeccable taste. Everything is gorgeous, from faucets to furniture. I'm really quite lucky.

A chill runs down my back, and goose bumps prickle my arms. It isn't from the weather, as Washington is clearly having one of its warm Octobers this year. I glance around.

Is someone watching me?

That, of course, is a ridiculous question. I'm not only a new neighbor moving in, but I'm moving into a murder house.

Everyone around here has to be curious about me. I've probably been the talk of the town since the Sold sign went up.

When they find out I'm a true crime podcaster and missing persons advocate, everyone will likely bore of me quickly. Why wouldn't I want to move in? This place is the ultimate PR move. That's what my critics online are already saying. They aren't entirely wrong—this will be great for my business—but I also want to see if I can solve this cold case and give closure to the surviving loved ones.

My followers are already going crazy, wanting details about the murder house I'm moving into. Several promotional posts have already gone viral.

It wouldn't surprise me if some of the neighbors have seen them. They should be excited to have me move in—I want to solve this mystery that's been hanging over their heads for the last two years. They should want that, as they knew both victims.

Nobody knows who killed Caroline Porter. Some suspect her husband, because he disappeared at the same time. Plus, it's always the husband. The stats in cases like this are astounding.

But they aren't one hundred percent.

That means Shane Porter could be alive and held captive somewhere. Unlikely, but possible. And I intend to get to the bottom of it.

What better way than to live in the Porters' house, living among their things? The cops have already been through the house—I'm sure they've left a mess for me to clean. They always do, that's one thing victims have told me time and time again when I've interviewed them.

I'm not moving into this house for the notoriety. I really do want to solve this case, and this is one way to get in the middle of the mystery that's unlike any other. I've already gotten heat online for my choice. Some think it's sick and twisted, but other people see it my way.

By stepping right into the middle of a case that's gone colder than the arctic, I can potentially figure out what happened and bring justice to this family. Maybe even find Shane alive.

What a miracle that would be. As someone who cares deeply for crime victims, nothing could be better.

Except, of course, solving the mysterious disappearance in my own family.

But that case is far colder than this one.

That's the case that sent me running across the country in the first place.

It's one I don't think will ever be resolved. Every time I help bring justice to another victim's family, I hope it will fill the hole in my heart. Fix my gaping wound.

Unfortunately, it never does.

Yet I can't help but hope *this* time will be different.

4

Fleur

Saturday, early evening

After Zorro finishes exploring the yard—including time spent running circles around it—I call him over to the front door. He looks at me expectantly, but I don't reach for the lock just yet.

I'm about to enter a house where a woman was murdered. Maybe also her husband.

And it's my home. Part of me thinks I'm crazy. I'm sure some of the neighbors agree with that assessment. I definitely felt curious, and even judgmental, gazes on me after I stepped out of the van.

They'll all change their tune after I solve this mystery. Then they'll be glad I moved in and got justice for their former neighbors.

The glut of true crime websites and podcasts indicate there should be more local interest in a young wife murdered in her own home and her missing husband. For some reason, that's not the case here. I've only found two media placements—a single small article in the town's online newspaper and the victim's obituary—neither of which revealed much. Beyond that... nothing.

"Are you the new neighbor?" The voice—friendly, male—comes from behind me.

I whip around to see the owner of said voice.

The guy looks to be about my age, tall and slender, with a short afro and a wide smile. "I'm Emmett Wycliffe."

Zorro runs over to him, sniffs, then wags his tail.

Emmett bends over to pat him, and Zorro licks his hand. "Aren't you sweet?"

I walk over to them. "That's Zorro."

"Love the name. The spot on his face looks like a mask." Emmett pats Zorro again before standing. "It's nice to meet your dog, but I'd love to meet you. What's your name?" He gives me another grin.

This guy is ridiculously good looking, especially when he smiles. It takes me a moment to hold out my hand to him. "I'm Fleur Bardot."

I throw in my last name since he told me his, although I've already forgotten it.

He shakes my hand with a firm grip. "Pleasure to meet you, Fleur. Are you named after any flower in particular?"

The question makes me hesitate. Most people I meet don't know that my name is French for flower. Almost every time I introduce myself, I have to explain that my name isn't *floor*. "My parents wanted to hang onto our heritage, so that's the name they picked."

"Nice." He nods in approval. "If you were to pick a particular flower, which one would you choose?"

"I've never been asked that before. You ask interesting questions."

"People tell me that a lot." He shrugs. "So, which flower would you want?"

"Definitely a sunflower."

"Why that one? Not that I'm judging."

"They're tall, strong, bright, and cheerful." I don't tell him this, but I actually have a tattoo of a sunflower on my shoulder.

"Good choice." He glances behind me toward the house. "How are you settling in?"

I chuckle. "I haven't even gone inside yet. Zorro and I literally just got here."

"Welcome to the neighborhood, then. Do you want some help moving your things in?"

"No, we're good. But thanks."

"Are you sure? You can be done in half the time."

"I'm sure." As tempting as the offer is, I'm not letting a stranger into my house. No matter how gorgeous he may be. Charm is deceptive. If Ian taught me anything, it was that.

"If you change your mind, give me a call."

"Okay..."

Emmett whips out his phone. "You'll need my number to do that."

Can't get anything past this guy.

We exchange numbers then say goodbye. He seems friendly enough, but something seems off about him. I can't put my finger on what, though. It might be nothing. I've gotten used to life in New York, and am used to looking at everyone with suspicion. My hometown suburb is the opposite of the enormous bustling city.

I wait until after he's out of sight before approaching my new front door. I'm looking forward to finding out more about what happened to the Porters after Zorro and I settle in. Living in their house with their things is the perfect way to find answers. If not within our walls, then from people who knew them personally. I should've asked Emmett if he knew them, but I can call him later if I don't run into him again.

As a neighbor, I'm going to have firsthand access to the people Caroline knew. Once they're comfortable with me, they'll let down their guards and tell me things they would never say to the police. Even if they're suspicious of me as a podcaster and author, I'm less of a threat than the law. I'm not an authority.

Zorro whines, reminding me we're still standing outside our new home.

I open the screen door, which squeaks loudly, then slide the key into the deadbolt. It turns easily, as does the lock on the knob. Now all I have to do is turn the handle.

My throat dries. I'm really doing this.

Zorro scratches at the door, clearly the more eager of us. I take a deep breath before opening the door. The evening's light shines in but doesn't reveal much.

I hesitate before reaching for a light switch. It flips easily, and several lamps around the room light up simultaneously.

The living room looks just like it did on the real estate website. Caroline and Shane Porter clearly had good taste. That much is obvious, even with everything covered in dust. Given how long this place was on the market, clearly most people have no interest in buying a home where someone was murdered, no matter how beautiful.

Their loss is my gain. Now I have a fully furnished house with a nice yard for my dog. After having to leave everything in the condo with Ian—even though we bought a lot of it together—it's such a relief to have a furnished home to move into. This one is much more my style, as it looks like it could be the showroom at an expensive department store. Ian always insisted on having things his way, even though I paid for half of what we bought. I stood up to him at first but quickly learned I didn't want to deal with his man-boy tantrums.

Now I don't have to put up with those any longer. Maybe the next woman who falls for his charm and lies can put him in line. He isn't my concern anymore.

Zorro is in full investigation mode, as now he's sniffing everything so intently his tail isn't even wagging. Usually, it never stops.

After a few sneezes, I open windows. I'm clearly going to have to clean before unpacking. Otherwise, the dust will win the battle against my allergies.

I leave Zorro to his sniffing and explore the rest of the house. All of the rooms have messes tucked behind furniture—clearly the detritus from the police search had been hidden rather than picked up for the listing photos. I'm sure the living room must too, thought I didn't notice at first glance. Given I got a beautiful, fully furnished home for a steal, I can't complain. So, I have some cleaning to do. Every place has its downside.

I peek into the office. Like everything else, it's exactly the same as it was on the website. I'm anxious to go through the drawers, not that I'm likely to find anything the police missed. But anything is possible. I have all the time in the world for this. Maybe I'll find a critical clue they overlooked.

Zorro comes into the room just as I'm opening the window. I pat his head on my way out.

I've gone through each room except one. I'm saving that one for last.

Not only is that the room that has the highest likelihood of holding answers, but I'm not sure I'm ready to go in it yet. I've been on the road for days and am beyond exhausted. I haven't even seen pictures, as the realtor who set up the listing didn't put *that* room on the site.

Curiosity burns, but I ignore it.

I need to bring in my belongings before it gets completely dark outside.

The murder room will have to wait—especially considering Mia still has its key.

5

Fleur

Saturday, late evening

I collapse onto the couch and pull my blankets up to my chin, barely able to keep my eyes open.

After Zorro and I went through the house, I brought out some of my things to make this place feel more like my home rather than a vacation rental. I even set up the king-sized bed with my sheets and comforter, but I couldn't bring myself to climb under the covers.

It didn't feel right.

I stripped the bed of my linens, leaving it a bare mattress. Now, I lay on the couch. I think it's a hide-a-bed, but I'm too exhausted to pull it out. After driving thousands of miles then spending today moving all my things inside from the van, I'm exhausted. Easiest to just sleep here as it is.

But I'm not sleeping. I'm trying—and failing—not to think about why the Porters left everything behind that now belongs to me.

A murdered wife and a missing husband. Is he still alive? Did the killer take Shane with him and kill him somewhere else? Did Shane follow him, and one of them killed the other? Or is it the obvious answer—that he killed his wife then fled to avoid facing the consequences?

My phone rings.

Who would be reaching out to me at this hour? If it's Emmett, I'm going to have to talk with him about boundaries.

I grab my phone from the coffee table then check the screen.

Mia. My best friend is spending the weekend camping with her boyfriend's family before the weather turns cold.

I accept the call. "Aren't you camping?"

She laughs. "Yeah, but a few of us are doing a supply run. I volunteered so I could check in on you. Did you make it to the house?"

"Got in a few hours ago. It's weird moving into a house with someone else's things."

"Yeah, but this is right up your alley! You're going to solve the mystery. I can feel it in my bones."

I glance around at all of the things the belonged to a dead woman and her possibly dead husband. It's going to be a huge undertaking. "We'll see."

"Your followers are going to *love* going through this with you every step of the way. You're already so successful, but this will take you to a whole new level!"

I wish I had her excitement. Maybe it'll return after a good night's sleep and time to recover from the road trip.

"We're about to go through the checkout line," Mia says. "I'll stop by Monday and see how you're doing. Sound good?"

"Sure." I stifle a yawn.

Mia whispers and laughs with someone before saying goodbye to me.

I end the call, and my eyelids grow heavy. Just as I'm about to drift to sleep, a sound jolts me awake.

Clink.

I sit up, clutching the blankets, trying to hear the noise over my pulse drumming in my ears. Maybe it was just the house settling. It hasn't had anyone living here in about two years. From what I understand, only listing agents have been in here to give a rare tour once in a while to people who had no interest in buying. It makes sense that Zorro and me moving in would cause the structure to shift and groan.

After a few more moments of silence, I lay back down and close my eyes.

Creak, creak.

That's definitely more than the house settling. I almost tell Ian to go check it out.

It's clearly going to take some time to break habits five years in the making. I hate that I keep thinking about him, but that'll stop soon. It has to. He's out of my life, and I'm all the better for it.

Clink.

This isn't the time to dwell on moving on from my ex. I have to figure out what's making those noises. It's all on me now. I'm the only person in the house. Can't rely on anyone else to do tedious tasks like these anymore.

After a deep breath, I look around for anything I could use as a weapon, just in case.

A fire poker. That should do the job. Better safe than sorry, even though it's probably just the house making noises that I'm not used to. I tiptoe over to the fireplace, grab the poker. Hold it close as I creep toward the bedrooms, where the sounds came from.

Creak, creak.

My breath hitches as I make my way down the hallway, ready to swing my weapon if needed. I keep Ian's face in my mind. His image inspires the anger I need to protect myself against a potential intruder.

I round the corner of the pitch black corridor. Definitely need to get a nightlight. Or five.

Shuffling noises sound at the end of the hall, as do a few creaks.

My pulse drums in my ears as I reach for the light switch. It's around here somewhere.

Somewhere.

My nails scratch against the paint, sounding like a bullhorn in the dark silence. If anyone *is* in the house, they're sure to know exactly where I am now.

Perfect.

Finally, I find the switch. Flip it up.

Light floods the hall, momentarily blinding me.

Zorro looks up from the corner, blinking rapidly, obviously not appreciating the sudden brightness.

Relief floods me, and my knees turn to rubber.

It was just my dog.

I hurry to him then wrap my arms around him. "You scared me, little buddy."

He licks my face.

Zorro usually sleeps in his bed through the night. It didn't even occur to me he'd be up and about, but it makes sense. We're in a new place. He did the same thing in all of the hotel rooms we stayed in along the way.

I make a mental note to set up a home security system so I don't have to worry about intruders again. That needs to be at the top of my priority list, along with about a dozen other things of equal importance. The responsibilities all fall on me now.

Another thing to get used to as a newly single person. At least I have my pup. I'm not completely alone.

My gaze lands on the door Zorro was sniffing at.

The murder room. I told Mia to lock it before I moved in. The other doors were all open, so the room's identity is no mystery—but everything inside is. I do plan to go inside. Eventually.

I have to. However, I want to go through everything else first. That's how I'll get to know the victims, by how they *lived*. I don't want to know about how she died until I get to know them first. Once I'm ready, my best friend will give me the key.

Zorro sniffs under the door again. I pat his head then walk toward the living room and call him to follow me.

Curiosity burns. Maybe I should get the key to the room from Mia sooner rather than later.

6

Fleur

Sunday, early morning

I bolt upright, gasping for air and twisting in my blankets. For one terrifying moment, I don't know where I am or why. Then it all comes flooding back to me—this is my new house, and all the unfamiliar things in it belong to me.

Once I relax and untangle myself from my blankets, I look around the living room. It's completely different in the bright morning light. Brilliant sunshine filters through the closed blinds, giving everything a cheery feel.

Or at least a *slightly* cheery feel. I'm not sure I'll ever be able to rid my mind of the knowledge of the murder that took place here. While I obviously knew what I was getting into when I bought this place, I definitely have mixed feelings. I'm not superstitious, nor do I believe in ghosts, but an event like that has to leave some kind of a mark on a place—strange energy or something. Or maybe it's nothing.

Guess I'll find out.

People die all the time. Probably in their homes more than anywhere else besides hospitals. Maybe retirement villas.

It's time this house gets new memories. There were probably plenty of good ones before the murder. In fact, I'll bet the good memories held within these walls far outweigh the bad by at least a thousand to one. Maybe even a million to one.

Those are good odds.

I need to focus on the task at hand, make a list of errands to run. Starting with groceries. The last thing I need is more prepackaged junk or fast food—that's all I've eaten over the last week. My body needs things that require refrigeration.

My stomach growls as if agreeing with the sentiment.

I gather everything I'll need for a shower. The bathroom attached to the primary bedroom still has bath products in the shower and cabinets. Literally everything is still here, even things I'd have thought someone would have removed. Things like shampoo, conditioner, body wash, toothpaste, toothbrushes, makeup, and other toiletries. Even prescriptions, which pique my curiosity. Nothing out of the ordinary—no antipsychotics or anything to indicate mental problems led to the murder. Although I'm sure the police would've confiscated stuff like that. Wouldn't they?

My mind returns to my hunger.

They didn't leave food in the kitchen, did they? Surely, someone would've removed that. My stomach roils at the thought of two-year old rotten food.

I might just lose my appetite if I check and find that. Maybe I should eat one more prepackaged meal before going grocery shopping then explore the kitchen later.

After I'm ready and on my way out, I can't help glancing at the one closed door. It could be anything from a bloody mess to a perfectly normal-looking room. Though, considering it wasn't pictured on the listing, it can't be great.

It's going to be so hard to ignore that room. Maybe I need to change my plan. Would it be so bad to start there instead of saving it for last?

My stomach rumbles, reminding me I need breakfast. I make my way to the van but stop cold before unlocking the door.

The front driver's side tire is flat.

So is the back one.

I stare in disbelief, glancing back and forth between them. My chest tightens as I make my way to the other side of the van.

Those tires have no air, either.

Somebody did this on purpose. There's no way all four of my perfectly good tires are flat when they got me across the country without a hitch.

Acid churns in my gut. I look around. Nobody's in sight. This place may as well be a ghost town.

I kneel and check the tire nearest me. There are no obvious gashes. If I'm lucky, that means the person who did this only let the air out and didn't destroy my property. How thoughtful of them.

Slam!

I jolt at the noise. That was a door shutting, and it was close.

Could someone be watching me?

I spin around, looking for anyone.

Nobody.

It was probably someone just stepping outside. And had nothing to do with my tires, which is what I need to turn my attention back to. I have too much to do today without having to worry about replacing a full set of car tires.

I check the rest of the tires, finding no visible slashes or gashes on those either. Why would someone go to all that effort? Could someone actually be upset about me moving in here?

First of all, what business would it be of theirs? Second, I'd think the neighbors would be happy. Having an abandoned house on the street only brings down the value of *their* homes. I'm not only going to fix up the place, but I'm literally bringing life back to it.

Given my line of work, I suppose I should have expected some people to be less than welcoming. I know more than most that everyone reacts differently to crimes. Some people shrink back, while others yell and scream. Apparently others seek vengeance on the innocent.

Hopefully whoever did this got it out of their system. Now I have to figure out how to air up the tires before the rims bend. *Then* I can get something to eat. Once I'm properly nourished, I'll find out what's in the kitchen.

Taking care of the tires is the type of thing Ian would've handled. Now it's on me. I'm not even sure if there's an air pump in the house—or whatever I would need to put the air back in the tires. I only know enough about cars to fill the gas and when to take it in to be serviced.

Why do I have a feeling I'm going to spend all morning researching this stuff online?

One thing I do know, there's a spare tire in the back of the van. Maybe there are other accessories in that compartment. It only takes a moment to get under the carpeting to the spare tire, and another moment to realize there's nothing else there. Not that I want to spend what's left of the morning manually pumping air into the tires.

The only other option is to get online and look for a company that will come to help me out—if that's even a thing. I have no idea, obviously. I'm so glad Ian isn't around to see me lost over this. He'd be laughing his head off at me.

No matter. I'm nothing if not resourceful. Even if there's no one who will come to the house, I'll find a solution. I didn't become the successful podcaster and author that I am by accident. If I could do that, I can take on four round pieces of rubber.

Right?

My first order of business is to see what's in the garage. There has to be something in there. I haven't explored it yet, but everything the former residents owned is still on the property. There must be something inside I can use to fix the tires.

I march over and stare at the door. There's a code box that I'm going to have to reconfigure later, but there's also a keyhole at the bottom of the large garage door. What are the chances the house key works?

There's only one way to find out.

I slide it in. It fits like a hand inside a glove. I turn, and it glides smoothly to the side.

Click.

It unlocked! Now all I need is to find an air pump.

I twist the handle then pull the large door open. It's loud enough to wake the dead, but at least I'm able to get inside without having to bother with going through the house.

Hopefully the Porters had an air pump, or I might be in over my head.

7

Fleur

Sunday, mid-morning

It's definitely my lucky day. Not only is the garage well organized and tidy, but everything is labeled and sorted by type. I quickly find not one but two air pumps—one manual and one automatic.

That's an easy decision. I choose the one labeled *compressor* and wheel it over to the minivan. Then I look around for an electric plug, finding one just outside the garage.

It almost reaches.

Almost.

So much for my good fortune. It isn't like I can move the van closer to the pump.

Maybe I need the manual one after all.

Ugh.

As I look for another electric socket—perhaps I missed one hiding behind some of the overgrown weeds—the tiny hairs on the back of my neck stand on end. Bumps form down my arms. I freeze in place.

Is someone watching me?

I spin around.

No one is in sight.

That doesn't mean a neighbor isn't peeking from behind blinds or a curtain. They all know this is a murder house, and it's been empty for two years. People must be curious about who's moving in. I know I would be. Not that I can ignore the fact that someone might not want me living here.

My flat tires are proof enough of that.

I may as well show them I'm friendly, so I give a big, obvious wave and a wide smile before returning to my search of an outdoor plug. After not finding one, I return to the garage for the manual air pump. It's better than nothing, even though I was so close to being able to use the compressor.

I pull the pump from its spot and give it a test in the garage. At least it pumps easily. With any luck, it won't take much time to fill up the four tires.

Then I see something even better. An entire tote full of extension cords.

I could seriously kiss Shane Porter. Now I don't have to manually pump four van tires after all.

Is it sexist of me to assume he's the one who organized everything in the garage? It might be, but the writing on the totes looks masculine. It was probably him.

Five minutes later, I'm filling the first tire. It swells beautifully, and the compressor even tells me when it reaches the ideal pressure. The little machine is louder than the garage door, but I don't care. I should be able to drive somewhere to eat in less than twenty minutes!

Soon, all of the tires are fully aired. None of them leak or lose pressure. I practically skip back to the garage to return everything where it belongs. After putting everything back in its place, I close and lock the garage door. Now my stomach is roaring like a bear robbed of her cubs.

Time for breakfast.

The tiny hairs on my neck stand straight again.

It's getting harder to ignore the likelihood of someone watching me. I refuse to let them think they're getting to me

Once in the van, I catch a glimpse of my reflection in the rearview mirror. Somehow I managed to get a streak of grease on my forehead stretching across to my hair.

So much for taking a shower earlier.

It only takes a few minutes to find a bakery. It's new since I moved away, but then again, a lot of things are. I left after graduating high school, and now I'm thirty. It would be more surprising if things *hadn't* changed.

The shopping center's parking lot is pretty full—the busyness a stark contrast from the sleepy neighborhood. When I step into Sally's Bakery, a bell chimes overhead and everyone turns my direction. Every single person in here is dressed up without a single hair out of place.

I forgot to wipe off the grease on my face, and my messy bun just drooped further. Even so, I muster a wide smile to everyone and step inside, feeling the stares of everyone on me.

Nothing like standing out on my first real day back. I recognize about half the faces. None of them look particularly happy to see me.

I try to ignore them as I get in line, but it's nearly impossible to focus on the menu while I absorb the customers' stares.

When I reach the counter, the woman at the register gives me a smile that doesn't quite reach her eyes. Her name tag tells me she's Sally. "Can I help you?"

"I'd like half a dozen donuts, please." Eating healthy will have to wait another meal.

"What kind?" Judgment oozes from her eyes as she spreads her palm toward the glass counters. The choices go on for days.

I pick out the ones that look the best.

She gives me a brief side-eye before grabbing a cardboard box and filling it with the sweets.

Whispers sound behind me. When I turn around, they stop. This isn't awkward at all.

I'd forgotten what it's like to be known only as sister of the dead girl. Not that anyone knows for sure that Lourdes *is* dead. They never found her body.

Kind of like Shane Porter, whose house I now live in.

Realization hits me like a bucket of cold water. Not only am I the sister of the dead girl, but now I live in the house of the murdered woman and her missing husband.

Everyone must know this fact. Word travels fast around here, and I'm sure even after all these years, nobody has forgotten about me.

I'm going to be an even bigger freak than I was all those years ago.

Maybe I should have thought through this more before buying a house that I'll never be able to sell. Too late now. I'm just going to have to make the best of the situation.

By the time Sally gives me the total, she doesn't even pretend to smile.

I reach into my purse for a card, but stop. The last thing I want is someone like her having sensitive information. I dig into my wallet for cash. Pay her with all ones. It's petty but at the moment I don't care. If she's going to glare at a paying customer like that, a little inconvenience isn't so bad.

Sally sighs loudly before tallying the change and handing it to me in pennies. Apparently two can play at that game.

"Thanks so much. This is *such* a cute bakery." I drop the change and another dollar bill into the tip jar before leaving without another word.

What a warm welcome back to town—first the tires, now this.

I'm just going to have to show people I'm an asset to the community. I'll be friendly and helpful, and hopefully I'll solve Caroline Porter's murder. Surely these people will appreciate that. Or they might hate me even more once they find out I'm a podcaster who will likely bring more attention to the town.

Time will tell.

By the time I return to my new neighborhood, it's more awake than before. One guy is raking leaves in his yard and two others are mowing their lawns.

Neither return my friendly wave and smile.

There are also three ladies gathered at the end of one driveway a few houses down from mine. They all watch me, still talking, as I make my way to my house and pull in. They inch closer to each other, glancing back and forth between each other and me.

Super subtle. Hardly even noticeable.

I wave and smile, but they only give me blank stares in return.

Wow. I can't get inside fast enough. The house is quiet. Zorro must not have heard me come in. I lean against the closed door and take a deep breath. People really aren't happy to see me.

It's too bad Emmett isn't around. I could use a friend right about now, and he's the closest thing I have to one around here since Mia lives across town. He must be an anomaly. So far, he's the only one willing to give me a chance.

I set the box of donuts on the kitchen table. Should've gotten some milk or mochas to go along with the breakfast, but I'm not going back outside for any reason short of a house fire.

No, I can't even think like that. With the way my morning has been going, that thought isn't too far out of the realm of possibility.

8

The Watcher

Hiding in safety

This is actually happening. Fleur Bardot has moved into the house. I was too chicken to speak up about my love for her when we were younger, then she moved away.

All the way across the country.

I've been kicking myself for years over that. If I had told her how I felt about her before she fled town, things could've ended up so different. We could be together now, and our children would be running around at her bare feet, pressing their little palms on her swollen belly.

It may not be our reality now, but it could be our reality soon.

She's back in town, and best of all, she's alone. I'd be lying if I said I wasn't afraid she'd move back with some guy and a ring on her finger. Her only companion now is a dog.

My love won't go unrequited forever.

We *will* be together. I just have to play this right. Unlike when I was a stupid kid.

The Bardot sisters were always the 'it' girls. There wasn't a straight guy in school who didn't fall for one—or both—of them at some point. Lourdes was too old for me, but not Fleur. She was always within reach, but I'd been too afraid of rejection.

If she'd rebuffed my affections…

Who knows what I would've done? I wouldn't want to hurt her, but a guy can't help what he does when his ego is wounded. That's something most women don't understand. They need to build up their men, then their men can keep them safe. That's the natural order of things.

Those two were always in a league of their own, with their natural blonde waves and perfectly golden skin. Legs that went on for days.

Lourdes and Fleur had to have been goddesses. I never believed in mythology until I laid eyes on them. The sisters could make a believer out of anyone.

It's too bad someone killed Lourdes. Well, technically nobody actually *knows* if she's dead. But how could she not be? The queen bee wouldn't give up her throne and adoring subjects on her own.

No. Obviously someone killed her. They brutally stole her life and brilliantly covered up the crime. In the fifteen years since she disappeared, nobody has come close to finding answers. Surely, it was a scorned lover or someone she brushed off. And that means literally anyone could be guilty. Lourdes turned down five guys for every one she didn't, and she made all the girls feel like dirt—and also plenty of adults.

I'm sure more people wanted her dead than didn't.

Now Fleur alone is this town's one goddess. Her sister is gone, never to be seen again.

That's why Fleur is obsessed with true crime. Her motivations are clear. In fact, her first podcast episodes were all about her precious sister. Now she only mentions Lourdes in passing. That makes sense, given that the case is as cold as the arctic.

I've listened to every one of Fleur's podcast episodes on loop, cycling through them repeatedly. Read her book multiple times. Every social media post, too. I've taken in every single word that beautiful woman has put forth to the world. I bet I know her better than she knows herself.

If she is a piece of art, then I'm the scholar whose job is to study her and catalogue every fact.

I'll never stop.

Not even after she belongs to me.

Which she will.

I'm going to see to that. I don't care what I have to give up or who I have to hurt in the process—even if it's her.

She *will* be mine. I will do whatever it takes to make that happen.

Nothing will get in my way.

9

Fleur

Sunday, late evening

After spending the whole day cleaning up the messes left by the police and crime scene investigators, now I'm watching a movie with Zorro—who's way too large to be a lap dog—sprawled across my thighs. But I can't pay attention to the storyline because I keep thinking about the flat tires, the awful stares people gave me at the bakery, and the whispers of my neighbors. The residents of my own hometown would rather I'd stayed away.

Nobody is going to push me out of my own home. They'll have to get used to the fact that I'm here to stay. I need to show them I'm an ally, not a problem. I'm not sure how to go about that since waving and smiling clearly isn't cutting it.

Maybe I should go door to door, bearing gifts to all the neighbors. Though if I do that, I'll have to get creative, or it will get expensive fast.

After rewinding the movie a dozen times, I finally give up.

There's no point trying to watch it when I can't pay attention. I get up and wander to the bedrooms, Zorro trotting next to me, his tail wagging. I stop in the doorway of the main bedroom. As much as I'd love to sleep on an actual mattress, the thought of lying in that bed gives me the heebie jeebies.

Nobody died in it, but I can't even bring myself to touch it. I'll keep sleeping on the couch until I replace the bed with one of my own. In fact, I'll probably replace everything in here. I can't imagine keeping any of it. A bedroom is so much more intimate than a dining room or den.

I want to get to know Caroline and Shane to figure out what happened to them, but this feels like too much. In fact, if I'm going to start digging around now, I need to pick a different room.

The office seems like a good place to start looking into things. It has a masculine look to it, so maybe I can learn something about Shane Porter's mindset. Did he love his wife and die alongside her, only to be taken somewhere else? Or did he commit the heinous act and run? Is there a third possibility where he's both alive and innocent?

The answer must be in there—the room that was so clearly his.

As I make my way down the hall, my gaze once again lands on the locked door. Was that Caroline's office? Given the home boasted two extra bedrooms, it would make sense for each of them to have their own working space. Maybe she was more traditional, and the room was a craft studio or something along those lines.

I can't even imagine what I'd do with a whole extra room all to myself. A soundproof podcasting area? Would I fill it with cork boards where I pin information about cases I'm looking into and string yarn from one connection to another until it looks like a spiderweb? I guess I don't have to imagine having an extra room anymore. I have several. And the possibilities seem endless.

After I figure out what happened to the previous residents, I'll have the entire house to fill as I please. It's mind-boggling but true. At some point, I'm sure I'll go from feeling like a houseguest to a homeowner.

I pull my gaze from the mystery door and step into the office. Even with there being almost no information out there about the murder, I already know what most people think. Everyone always suspects the husband. Statistics show it's true in most cases, but not all, cases. The man who decorated this room *could* be as much of a victim as his wife.

He might be alive out there somewhere. It's always a possibility until someone finds his body, and if I'm going to be a good investigator, I have to keep an open mind.

I take a seat in the leather chair behind the desk and look around the office, as Shane must have done so many times. He'd decorated in colors of muted browns and grays, and there are several framed sports car pictures. They aren't professional photos, given the busy backgrounds, making me think he took them all himself.

Car enthusiast and photographer.

That's the first observation—of many more to come, I'm sure—I jot into my favorite notes app.

The walls tell the story of what Shane enjoyed and wanted to show off. Interesting that there aren't any pictures of his wife in here. Not even on the desk. Did he prefer cars to her? Or did he figure he could simply walk down the hall if he wanted to see the woman he married? Unless the cops took those, but it seems unlikely.

Another note into the app.

I reach for the top drawer to see what clues hide in there.

Tap, tap.

That's not Zorro. It came from the outer wall—from outside. Like something bumping against the house.

I hold my breath and sit still, waiting to hear it again.

Nothing.

I reach for the top drawer again just as I did a moment ago.

Silence.

It was probably something innocent, like a raccoon or squirrel. I never heard those in the New York apartment but always did when I was growing up. I'm just not used to the wildlife anymore.

Not that I can blame myself for being a little jumpy. I'm not only living alone now, but someone died in this house. And nobody in town seems happy about me being back.

My skin crawls at the thought.

Perhaps I bit off more than I can chew with this place. But I don't regret my decision. This place is much bigger than where I lived before, and now I'm not waiting on some loser who only wanted to string me along with untruthful promises of a future marriage and family.

What more could I ask for than this?

Tap, tap, tap.

There still has to be a rational explanation. Pipes, for instance. I've had a shower today and done a load of dishes. That's more action than the pipes have seen in the last two years.

The pipes must be what I'm hearing.

I get up from the comfy chair and press my ear against the wall where the noises were coming from.

Nothing.

I move around, trying different parts of the wall, as best I can in an office full of shelves, books, and framed car photos.

If it isn't the pipes, there has to be a logical explanation for the tapping—tree branches, animals, or neighbors making noise that sounds closer than it is.

I'm just being silly—to be expected, as I'm still not used to this house. Every home has plenty of oddities to adjust to. Before long, things that seem strange now will become background noise.

Tap.

I throw my hands in the air. What *is* that noise? It still sounds like it's coming from the outer wall. Could someone be out there now?

Considering what happened with my tires earlier today, it's not out of the realm of possibility. If someone was willing to deflate those, why not sneak into the backyard and mess around outside a lit-up window?

I turn off the light, take a deep breath, then tiptoe over to the window, lifting one of the blinds slightly. It's already dusk. Everything is dark and shadowy. It's impossible to make out details.

In other words, it's the perfect time for someone to sneak around and scare the new neighbor.

The first thing I need to do tomorrow is set up an alarm system, or at least a doorbell camera. Anything that would deter people. For all I know, all of this is just kids pulling pranks. I was certainly guilty of pulling a few when I was young and bored.

Plus, there must be rumors about this place being haunted between the murder and it being abandoned. The kids wouldn't be old enough to remember, so I'm probably a curiosity—the woman crazy enough to move into a murder house.

I release the blind then step back. I'm on edge and need a little time to show everyone I'm no threat.

Tap, tap.

That's it. I'm done sitting back.

Time to go outside and see what's making the noises once

and for all. Whether it's a raccoon, kids, or a murderer, I'm going to give them a piece of my mind.

10

Fleur

Sunday, late evening

On my way outside, I grab the fire poker from the other night. It isn't ideal, especially since I have to use my phone as a flashlight, but it should work. This thing could inflict some serious damage if I swing it hard enough.

Everything is quiet out here. Not to mention dark. It takes my eyes a moment to adjust after being in the bright office. The moon overhead is only a sliver, so that doesn't help much. I consider turning on the porch light but can't let anyone know I'm out here.

In fact, I don't bother turning on my phone's light. I might be able to get around without it, as I've walked around back here a few times. I mostly know where everything is, but it would also be easy to bump into something.

I tiptoe toward the other side of the house, keeping my fingertips on the brick.

There isn't any noise, not even a hint of the incessant tapping. It was definitely coming from outside. I wasn't imagining that. There's no way it was coming from the room.

Unless it was coming from inside the walls.

No. I don't want to even think about that possibility. Animals living in the walls is more than I can deal with right now, although given how long this house has been empty, it's a strong possibility.

Hopefully I'll find something out here. Then I can chase it away and move on with my night, putting this behind me.

That's a much better thought than animals in the walls. Or worse, a person out here.

I round the corner to the side of the house where the office is located. My breath hitches and I stop to listen.

Something rustles near where the house and fence meet. Or is that my imagination?

A shiver runs down my spine. I feel exposed. Sure, I have this fire poker but what if someone is close by and has a gun?

I have to be brave. Scratch that, I *am* brave. How many people would travel across the country with only what they could fit into a van and move into a murder house?

Maybe I'm not so much brave as I am desperate.

Either way, I need to find out what's going on. If someone is messing with me—and given what happened to my tires, they are—I need to stand up to them, even if I'm shaking inside.

I take a deep breath and move toward the fence, clinging to the cold metal of the poker so hard my fingers ache.

Rustle.

The poker shakes in my grip.

"Who's there?" I demand, keeping my voice steady. With any luck, I sound surer than I feel.

No response.

"Show yourself."

Please don't. The last thing I want is to get into a fight with someone who probably has the advantage.

Rustle.

My mouth goes dry. I can't give into my fear. "I know you're there. Just tell me who you are and what you want."

Something skitters at my feet.

I barely hold in a yelp as I scramble to turn on my phone's light.

A possum. Its eyes glow in the light as it runs past my feet and toward the main part of the yard. Two tiny possums chase after it.

My knees turn to rubber as the realization runs through me. The noises were from a mama and her babies. That was all. It's not a person trying to scare me... or worse.

Gasping for air, I lean against the house and try to regain my bearings. After a few moments, I release a laugh. I'm not sure if it's from relief or from acting like a scared kid.

This whole thing reminds me of a time when my friends and I left a slumber party one night and poked around a house we all believed belonged to a witch. We creeped around, scared half to death she would jump out and boil us for dinner.

Looking back, the poor woman probably wasn't that different from me now. She lived alone in a house that desperately needed repairs, and her only friends ran around on four legs. Though she had a multitude of cats, whereas I have only Zorro.

Once I'm sure my legs will carry me back inside, I step away from the house and shine the light around the ground.

Something metallic catches my eye on the sill of the office window.

I step closer. It's some kind of jewelry.

A necklace.

Not just any necklace. I recognize it.

My legs wobble. Everything other than the heart-shaped locket disappears around me.

It can't be.

Except there isn't another explanation.

This necklace disappeared fifteen years ago. Right along with my sister.

11

Fleur

Sunday, late evening

It takes me a few moments to gather the courage to pick up the locket. Part of me wonders if I should leave it and let the police take it.

What if it's evidence? Except nobody cares about Lourdes anymore. Her disappearance is ancient history, her case colder than the ice.

Even so, I pick it up with my sleeve so as not to touch it. Hold it up to the light. It isn't varnished, almost like someone has been taking care of it all this time. The locket shines like new, bringing me back to our childhood home.

I can smell pot roast cooking—Dad's favorite meal—and see in front of me my beautiful older sister with her favorite necklace resting over her shirt. It's a golden locket given to her by our grandmother, Mimi Perle. It had been hers as a girl, and with Lourdes being the oldest granddaughter, she got it.

I'd always been jealous of not only the golden piece of jewelry but my sister's close relationship with our grandma. I only missed out because I'd been born a couple years too late.

Now the locket is in my possession. It's not how I wanted to get it.

How is this even possible? Is Lourdes alive and well, playing one of her pranks on me? Or was this a keepsake from her killer, now sending me a message?

My blood chills at that thought.

I shine my light around the yard. A killer could be watching me.

Choking back a gasp, I run back around the house still clutching the necklace through my sleeve.

Once back inside, I lock the door and close the blinds. Zorro circles my feet, but I don't have the wherewithal to give him any attention.

I drop my find on the coffee table, staring at my dead sister's necklace. It feels like a viper about to strike.

It *has* to be the family heirloom. But there's no logical reason for it being where I found it.

Lourdes has been gone fifteen years—she had no reason to walk away from her life. At first, the police wouldn't take her disappearance seriously, saying she was a runaway who'd soon be back. They'd told our distraught parents to give it forty-eight hours and if she hadn't returned by then, to come back to file a report.

Cops should know how vital the first hours of a disappearance are. They're crucial, not only for finding leads but because of the ticking clock. Most victims are murdered within that short window. But in small towns where nothing bad ever happens, it was more comfortable to believe she'd left of her own volition. At the time, their reaction made sense. But it doesn't ease my grief. Lourdes might have been found, saved, if the authorities had taken the report seriously.

A lump forms in my throat.

Nothing is going to bring back my sister, not even finding her locket. She's gone. Lourdes Alison Bardot loved her life and would have never left it of her own free will. My sister was the queen bee at school—most everyone either wanted to be her or wanted to be at her side. She was the kind of girl who even got romantic interest from some of the teachers, back when that sort of thing was seen more as taboo than abuse. The attention was the fuel that kept her going every day.

There were, however, also plenty of people who would've been more than happy to see her disappear. For every person who adored her, there was one who was jealous and another who had been burned by her. Anyone who ever crossed Lourdes's path came to regret it. More than a few hated her.

My sister could be the sweetest person or the most vindictive—it depended on how one treated her. But of course, nobody likes to speak ill of the dead, so for the last fifteen years, all anyone talks about is her sweet side.

Her sweet side isn't what got Lourdes killed.

The song "Sweet but Psycho" has always made me think of her. It could've been written about her.

I know full well my older sister is dead. Someone didn't want her ruling the halls of our high school, so they made sure she couldn't. In the most permanent way possible.

And they're still walking free.

I close my eyes and take a deep breath. It takes me a few moments to orient myself and come back to the present moment. I need to open the locket and see the proof that this is my sister's.

Even though I know it is.

I shouldn't risk my prints getting on it, but they are most likely already there. Sometimes when Lourdes wore another necklace, I secretly wore this one. It did belong to *our* grandma, after all. She would've wanted me to enjoy it, too. At least that's what I told myself at the time. I wouldn't do that now, obviously, but teenage me was definitely jealous of my sister's popularity, charm, and beauty. Not to mention the power she held over people.

Not that I'd have admitted it then.

I don't want any of it now. Not after I've seen the damage it can cause. I'm more than happy to keep to myself in my house, getting word out about missing person cases. Nothing makes me happier than to see a family get the answer they've been searching for, even though it's rarely the answer they *want*. Like me, they know their loved one is likely gone, but there's something to be said for closure. I should know.

It's eluded me for a decade and a half.

Hopefully this locket will help provide answers.

A lump forms in my throat. I never thought I'd see this again, or the pictures inside. It's like seeing Lourdes again, in a small way. This was her necklace. She loved it and wore it so often that anyone who knew her would recognize it right away.

It would be easier to open with my bare hands, but I can't risk that. Whoever left it for me to find clearly wants that.

I'm not about to fall into anyone's trap. If anybody knows how true crime works, it's me. My life and career revolve around it.

Finally, I manage to get it open.

I can hardly believe my eyes. Tears blur my vision. I blink them away, only to have more return in their place. Instead of fighting them, I wait a minute and let them flow freely until I can finally focus.

The inside of the locket hasn't changed in the last fifteen years. There's a picture of Lourdes and me as children on one side of the locket, and one of our grandma as a teenager on the other side.

The necklace has been perfectly preserved for all these

years. It hasn't been in the elements at all, not on a decomposing corpse.

Has it been with the killer all this time?

If so, why did that person leave it for me to find? And how did they know to find me *here* in this house?

That's the more pressing question.

12

Fleur

Monday morning

After last night, I'm exhausted. Even so, I can't sleep another moment on the couch. I need to clear out the bedroom and make it my own. The sooner the better.

If I'm going to get anything done today, I need caffeine. While I do have groceries now, I don't have a coffee maker—that needs to be shoved to the top of my to-do list. I'm definitely not returning to Sally's Bakery for my morning fix.

I feed Zorro then go outside while he's distracted. Before I reach the van, I stop.

A woman about my age stands at the edge of my driveway, staring at me. With her dark hair pulled back, I can clearly see her face. Her gorgeous brown eyes are big as dinner plates as she takes me in.

"Can I help you?" I ask.

Her expression softens. "I... you... for a moment I... I thought you were her."

It takes me a moment to realize she means Caroline. We both have long blonde hair, but that's where the similarities end. Though it was obviously enough to jar my poor neighbor.

"When you stepped out of the front door, it was like she was back. But she's gone. It's been two years."

"I didn't mean to upset you. Were you close to her?"

"Caroline was my best friend."

Her words gut me. "I'm so sorry. I know how hard it is to lose someone in such a traumatic way."

"You do?"

"My sister disappeared fifteen years ago. Presumed dead." My voice catches in my throat. "Exactly half my life. She's been gone as long as she was in my life. Sometimes even now when I see someone resembling her, for a split second I wonder if it's her."

It's so weird opening up to a stranger, but she seems to uniquely understand what I've been through. I definitely recognize her spooked expression.

"Wait." The woman's expression sharpens. "Are you Lourdes's sister?"

We're back to that—I'm not me, I'm the dead girl's sister.

"That was probably rude. Forget I said anything." She looks away.

"No, it's fine." It's completely not fine, but whatever. "Yes, Lourdes was my sister. Did you know her?"

She looks back at me. "In passing. Caroline and I were in the grade above her. I think we had a class together, but we didn't run in the same circles. Sorry. I'm Darby."

I extend my hand. "Nice to meet you. I'm Fleur. I just moved in."

Her eyebrows pop up. "Your name is Floor?"

"No, *Fleur*. It's French for flower." Sometimes I really think I should change my name.

Her face reddens. "Sorry. That was a dumb question."

"Don't worry about it. I get that all the time—always have. My parents moved here from France and wanted to keep the culture alive in my sister and me. Giving me a name that sounds like floor made me want nothing to do with our history, and now my name is one of the only French words I know." I change the subject. "Where do you live?"

Darby points toward the end of the road. "My husband Troy, our two daughters, and I live on the corner."

"How old are your girls?"

"Ashley's three and Emma's one."

"Cute. Where are they now? Daycare?"

"No, I homeschool them. They're inside with Troy while he gets ready for work." Her gaze darts around, and she fiddles with her hair. "How's the house? Is it, uh… is their stuff still inside?"

"Yeah. I hope that isn't too weird for you, but I needed a place that was already furnished. I moved across the country and could only take what fit into the van."

"Makes sense." Darby nods. She chews on her lower lip.

Is she debating whether to say something?

Maybe she wants one of Caroline's belongings. The two of them were best friends, after all.

"Did you want to look around?" I ask. "You two were close, so I'm sure having something of hers would be comforting."

Her hand goes to her heart. "Really? You'd do that?"

"You have more of a right to her things than I do. Come on." I wave toward the house.

She glances at her fitness watch. "I have a few minutes before Troy has to leave."

I lead her inside, where Zorro runs around the corner and licks our guest repeatedly.

"Down! Stop!"

Thankfully, he stops.

I turn to Darby. "I'm so sorry."

She laughs. "Don't worry about it. I love dogs."

"Do you have one?"

Her expression falls. "No. Troy thinks they're too messy."

"What about what you think?"

Darby shrugs then looks around. "It's like they just stepped outside. I feel like she could walk in at any moment."

"I'm glad to hear you say that, because I feel more like a guest than an owner."

Darby glances over at the couch, where a lot of my luggage is piled. "Once you make it your own, I'm sure it will all be good. If you need any help, let me know."

"Are you sure?"

"Of course. What are neighbors for? I can even make an extra serving of dinner and bring it over for you tonight."

"Wow, thanks. I really appreciate that. I'm not used to such hospitality."

"Where did you move from?"

"New York City."

"Let the Wilsons show you some good old-fashioned hometown hospitality."

"That's a mouthful, but I'll take it. Speaking of taking things, what of Caroline's do you want? I haven't spent any time in their bedroom. Maybe she has a piece of jewelry that was special to her that you'd like?"

"There *is* that one bracelet." She doesn't look so sure.

"Perfect!" I wave her toward the hall and to the primary bedroom.

Darby goes straight to the jewelry box, obviously knowing where her best friend kept it.

I remain by the door, still not comfortable with the room. "You don't happen to need a queen sized bed, do you?"

She glances over at me. "You don't want it?"

"No, it's the first thing I'd like to replace."

"Troy and I have been talking about getting a new bed, but we're on a budget."

"It's yours. Take it as soon as you can."

"Thanks so much. I can hardly believe how generous you are." She clasps a bracelet onto her wrist.

"You're helping me out. If you take the bed, I don't have to hire someone to pick it up."

"When you buy a new bed, the company should offer to take this for you."

I should probably know that. One more thing to learn as a single woman. "Even the frame and headboard?"

"You don't want those either?"

"None of it."

"Gosh, I can't wait to tell Troy. He won't believe it. I'll have to make you dinners for a month to pay you back for your kindness."

"It isn't necessary—though I'll never turn down free food."

Darby closes the little drawer in the jewelry box. "Let's exchange numbers so we can figure out a time for us to take this bed off your hands."

I recite my number, and she texts me.

> UNKNOWN
> This is Darby Wilson.

> FLEUR
> Thanks, Fleur Bardot.

I text her back my full name because nobody can ever spell it—how many times have I seen it spelled Floor Bardo?—then we head back to the front door.

She stares at the living room like she's seen a ghost. I'm sure it feels that way after her best friend died so long ago yet her house is exactly the same as it had been.

Finally she turns to me. "How do you like the house?"

"It's an adjustment. I haven't had much time to settle in yet. I'm still trying to get used to new sounds at night. I'm sure you know how that goes. It'll be such a relief when this place feels like home."

"I bet. Well, I'd better get going before I make Troy late for work. Thanks again for everything. I can't tell you how much it means to be back in here. In a way, it's like getting to be with Caroline again."

"I'm glad I could help. Let me know when you want to pick up the bed. Will it be today?"

Darby laughs. "Eager much? I'll see what I can do."

"I can help you move it, if you don't want to wait on Troy. We can probably fit it all in my van once it's broken down."

"You don't have to do that. It looks like you have enough to do around here."

"Isn't that the truth?"

She waves, lets herself outside, then closes the door behind her.

After all my other interactions with people, it's hard to believe I might actually have a friend in town. Other than Mia.

At least it's a start.

Now that I'm alone, I need to figure out what to do about the locket necklace. The right thing would be to hand it over to the police.

Except that's the last thing I want to do with it.

13

Fleur

Monday morning

D<i>ing-dong!</i>
Zorro runs around between the door and me, eager to see who's here.

Can't I catch a break for even ten minutes? I carefully hide the necklace in my pocket and trudge over to the door to peek outside.

My annoyance melts away. It's Mia.

I throw open the front door and wrap my arms around my best friend. Even though we haven't seen each other in person for a few years, suddenly it's as if we were never apart. I'm not sure how long we cling to one another—it could be one minute or fifteen.

Time ceases to exist with her.

She gives me her wide, bright smile after we pull apart. "I've missed you so much!"

"Pretty sure I've missed you more."

"Obviously. You've been across the country forever. How's Ian? Sobbing on the floor, unable to function?"

I can't help smiling. "I wish. No, he's probably staring lovingly into his own reflection as we speak. That's the only thing he cares about."

"Seems to be your type."

My mouth falls open. "Not true."

She laughs. "*So* true."

Time for a change of subject. "How was the weekend? You must be pretty serious about this guy to go camping with his family."

"They're really cool, actually. I think I might like his sister more than him."

"Don't think about replacing me," I tease. "I'm your best friend."

"How could I forget?" She steps inside, petting Zorro, and looks around. "You haven't redecorated yet?"

"I only got in Saturday night, and I've had to put away the messes the police left."

"Right. Is it weird living in a murder house? Or is it just another day in the life a famous true crime podcaster?"

"Who are you calling famous?"

Mia lifts a brow. "My bestie, of course. Your podcast was in the top 100 overall last time I checked."

"That's only because I've been talking up this move. Word has spread through the true crime community. Everyone is curious. The buzz will die down eventually."

"Stop being modest. It isn't *just* because you're moving here to solve a crime. If nobody was following you before that, word wouldn't have spread in the first place."

I shrug. While I do love my job, one thing I don't like is conversations like this. I'm definitely not famous—nobody will be stopping me in public for a selfie or autograph any time soon—but I have made a name for myself in my little niche. It's big enough to pay the bills, but I'll never be a household name and I'm fine with that. Glad, actually.

Mia pulls a key from her purse. "Sure you don't want the key to the murder room?"

I stare at it. It would be nice to have on hand should I decide I'm ready to go in for a look.

She gives me a playful smirk, as if reading my thoughts. "All you have to do is say the magic word."

"What's the magic word?"

"'Gimme.'"

"I'll think about it."

"You're no fun." She drops the key back into her purse. "Found anything interesting while cleaning the cops' messes?"

"Not really. You know what's weird about this place?"

"Other than the fact that someone was murdered here?" Mia glances around like she's looking for something. Like the dead body is still lying around. I may be the crime podcaster, but I swear she has more of a morbid curiosity than me.

"There are hardly any pictures of the couple around here. Most people have framed photos on display, you know? The only pictures I've seen of them are online—and there isn't much there. It's strange."

"They were probably taken as evidence. I'm surprised you haven't thought of that."

"All of them?"

"What do I know about murder evidence?" Mia asks. "I sell houses for a living."

"Exactly. *You* should know that most people have photos of their life all around."

"Most people, sure. But not everyone. You'd be surprised. There seems to be a trend lately of people not wanting to see their own faces all over their homes."

"Seriously? You have to be kidding me."

"Why would I joke about that?"

"No idea. You want something to eat? Unfortunately, I don't have much yet."

"Nah, I'm fine. Can I look around? I'm curious."

"You didn't go through everything before?" I study her, trying to make sense of everything she's said about this place and the odd trend of not putting up pictures. Maybe I'm getting old and just don't understand young people now.

No, I'm only thirty. It'll be a while before I turn into a fuddy-duddy.

My best friend gives me a knowing look. "I only had one client interested in this place, and she didn't want a virtual tour. What reason did I have to come in here?"

"How'd you get the keys?"

"The lockbox on the door."

I grab a donut for myself then give her the grand tour.

When we get to the primary bedroom, she marches in ahead of me before turning around. "You're not coming in?"

"This room gives me the creeps."

"Why?" She plops down on the bed and glances around, running her fingers over the mattress. "Did you remove their linens?"

"Yeah. How did you know?"

"I, uh, well... I assume the cops didn't take it. She wasn't killed in here. Plus, everything else is dusty. And they don't go with the rest of the decor."

Her answer doesn't sit right with me, but I brush it aside. I'm probably on edge from being in this room.

Mia's gaze roves over the two dressers. "If you don't like this room, why not put your own blankets on here? Make it yours."

"I've already found someone to take the bed off my hands. Soon I'll have my own bed to sleep on."

"You did? Who's taking it?"

"A neighbor who was friends with Caroline."

"I could've taken it. Sometimes I need furniture to stage houses I'm selling."

"Good to know. I'll keep that in mind when I get rid of other stuff."

"Thanks. Who got the bed?"

"Her name is Darby."

A scowl crosses Mia's face briefly, but it's gone almost as soon as it appeared.

"You know her?"

"Of course. This is a small town."

"You don't like her?"

"It isn't that." Mia glances at her fitness watch and leaps to her feet. "I hardly know the woman. But she seems nice enough."

"I thought so. She offered to bring me dinner."

"That's sweet. Are you sure you don't want to check out the mystery room really quick? Might be easier with a friend by your side. I have a little time before my next showing."

"Maybe another time, but I think I'll take the key just in case I change my mind about the room."

Disappointment washes over her face. "Really?"

"Yes." I hold out my hand.

"You don't want your bestie to explore with you?"

"I don't even want to look by myself, but I'd like the option. If I'm going to try and solve the mystery, I need access to the room. I might decide to go in on a whim in the middle of the night."

"And I'll come over no matter the time."

I inch my open palm closer to her.

Her mouth curves down as she digs out the key then drops it onto my hand. "I'm happy to explore with you anytime, day or night."

"I'll keep that in mind."

"You don't want me to join you?" Hurt shines in her eyes. "I helped you get into this place, knowing that it could be huge for your podcast."

Guilt stings. "It isn't that. I just... I don't know when I'll be ready to go in that room. There's a *lot* to go through in the whole house. It's two people's lives, and I have to handle it with care. If I mess anything up, there's no going back. I'm also not entirely sure how I'm going to do this. Documentary style with a video? Or report later? There's a lot to think about, and I'm not sure yet. I want it to be just right."

Not only that, but I may have a more important murder to solve. I'm tempted to pat my pocket with the necklace in it, but I don't want to draw attention to it.

Mia's expression softens. "That makes sense. Sorry to put pressure on you. I got a little over-excited about the thought of you solving the mystery. You really would be famous then. Oprah would want an interview with you. Can you imagine?"

"I think that's going a little far, but it might draw more attention to my podcast and books."

"Exactly! You definitely deserve the notoriety." Her watch beeps and she glances at it again. "Ugh, I have to go—big showing. Meet up for drinks soon? I could introduce you to Donovan and Cleo. You'll adore her."

I laugh. "Should I find it concerning that you seem to like your boyfriend's sister more than him?"

"We just get along. He was probably drawn to me because we're so similar."

"If she's like you, I'm sure she's great."

Mia wraps her arms around me. "It's so good to have you back. I knew I missed you, but I didn't realize how much until now. Don't leave again."

"Pretty sure I can't. I'll never be able to sell this place."

"I'd be lying if I said that thought didn't cross my mind when I talked you into buying."

I give her a playful shove. "I'm sure it had nothing to do with the commission."

"You got a discount, I'll have you know."

"I remember. It never gets old teasing you."

"Same."

We head outside, but I return to the house to grab my sunglasses. I hadn't expected it to be so bright in October. When I turn to Mia, her eyes are wide and color drains from her face.

"Are you okay?"

She stumbles over her words. "I... you... for a moment I thought Caroline was walking out the door."

Exactly what Darby said.

Something weird is going on here, and I intend to find out what.

I march over to my best friend. "What are you hiding from me?"

She stumbles back, bumping into her shiny, red Mercedes.

"You need to tell me."

Mia closes her eyes for a moment. "Okay. We should go inside and sit down first."

My stomach roils. What am I about to find out?

14

Fleur

Monday, late morning

Zorro curls at my feet as soon as Mia and I sit at the kitchen table with steaming mugs of tea—probably expired since I found the bags in the cabinets. But right now, I don't care about old chamomile.

I stare at my friend expectantly as she glances around the room.

"Care to fill me in?" I tap the table with a chipped nail.

Mia turns her attention back to me and sighs. "Caroline and I became friends after I helped her and Shane buy this house. We hit it off pretty quickly. Now I realize it's because she made me think of you."

"Why hide it from me?"

She picks at a hangnail. "I felt bad about how quickly we became close. You were all the way across the country, struggling to find your place in a massive city, and here I was finding a new best friend. I didn't want to hurt your feelings."

It takes me a moment to find my voice. "She was your best friend?"

"I'm sorry. She was here—in person. You and I only talked on the phone and through texts. Ian kept you so busy, and we were growing apart."

"And you found someone so much like me, it was easy to replace me."

Mia glances back at me, her eyes wide. "Nobody could replace you."

I snort. "Caroline was so similar to me, seeing me here was like seeing a ghost."

"It wasn't like that."

"No?" I stare her down.

"She was easy to talk to, and she wasn't happy in her marriage. I was the perfect person to talk to."

"Because you sold them their house?"

Mia shakes her head.

"What, then?"

"I was her only friend who wasn't part of their church."

"What does that have to do with anything?" I sip my tea, trying to calm my nerves. Why would Mia think she had to hide this from me? Did she really think I expected her to not make friends locally with me gone?

"From what Caroline described, it wasn't just a run of the mill church—the members are controlling. They would kick someone out for getting a divorce. The whole community was all she knew, and she feared losing everything if she walked away."

"I still don't understand why you felt the need to keep that from me."

"I'm telling you now."

"What else have you hidden from me?"

She frowns.

"There really *is* more." I gulp down the rest of my tea.

"I brought you here to solve my friend's murder. Someone from her church had to have done it."

"If they did, why haven't the police found them?"

Mia's brows draw together. "Because almost everyone on the force is part of it. They would all cover for each other."

I rub my temples. "Are you sure? If there was a controlling religious group here in town, I'd remember that."

"A lot has changed in the years you've been gone."

"Apparently. When did this group take over the town?" I try to keep the sarcasm out of my tone, but the exasperated look in her eyes tells me I didn't do a good job of it.

"They haven't taken over the town, but they've gained more influence as the group has gotten bigger. It was small when we were in high school. They didn't even have a building back then. According to Caroline, they met in someone's house before renting space in the community center."

My mind spins, trying to make sense of it all. "So, you think a member of this church killed her and other members are covering it up?"

"It explains why there has hardly been any coverage in the news, and why it hasn't been solved."

"Why would Shane disappear if he had people in authority to cover for him?"

"They could've killed him too."

"Now you aren't making any sense. If Caroline wanted to leave the marriage, they would be on his side."

Mia sips from her mug. "Unless she managed to talk him into leaving the church. Her main problem with Shane was the control he exerted over her because of what they were taught by the other members. They were in love and trying to have a baby at one point. He might've been willing to leave with her, especially if he was uncomfortable with the control the church made him exert over her. If that was the case, those people could've killed both of them."

"This is bananas. You realize that, don't you?"

"You don't understand the influence the Beacon of Truth Fellowship has on its members. I know you've come across cults in your time spent on unsolved missing people—that's what we're dealing with. People obsessed with power, who don't want to give that up. You know what I'm talking about. These high control groups are no joke."

"I'm aware of that."

"Then you should see my theory makes sense. They had to have killed Caroline and Shane—there's no other explanation. We *need* an outsider to solve this case!"

"I'm an outsider?" I exclaim. "Do I need to remind you I grew up here? Or did you forget we were best friends in high school? You moved here during our sophomore year—you're technically the outsider."

Her face flushes red. "You've been gone for the last twelve years! Everything has changed. You have no idea."

"I need some space."

"What?"

"Please, can we finish this conversation later?" I rise and gesture toward the door. "I need some time to think."

"Are you at least still going to look into the murders?"

"Of course I will."

"Fleur..." Mia pleads with her eyes.

I trudge to the entrance and open the door. "We'll talk later."

She trudges over. "I'm really sorry."

"I appreciate that. I just need some space to process this. Besides, didn't you say you have a big showing?"

"Right. I should get to that." She steps outside.

I close the door between us.

She and Caroline were best friends? During all of our conversations over the years, Mia didn't mention her even once. Now she expects me to solve the murder?

I lean against the door, slide to sitting, then pinch the bridge of my nose.

Zorro trots over and licks my hand. I pat him absentmindedly as I try to make sense of everything. Shane and Caroline were part of a cult. My supposed best friend was actually best friends with Caroline, who apparently wanted out of her marriage. And Darby down the street thought *she* was Caroline's best friend—while I thought I was Mia's best friend.

Were Mia and Caroline hiding their friendship from everyone? Or just Darby and me?

I pat my pants where the necklace is. "Sorry, Lourdes. Your mystery is going to have to wait a little longer. At least I know not to trust the police with your locket. For now, let's find out what's behind that locked door."

Zorro follows alongside me as I make my way to the murder room. I hesitate before taking the key and sliding it into the lock.

It turns easily. I remove it before slowly opening the door.

The sight takes my breath away.

The key slips from my grip, bounces on the floor.

Shane and Caroline were clearly keeping a secret from both of her best friends. Or their friends are keeping it from me.

One thing is sure—I didn't expect to see *this*.

15

Fleur

Monday, noon

I can hardly move, hardly breathe as I stare at the room, clinging to the door frame.

None of this was mentioned in any of the reports I read online. It's possible the police are keeping it close to the vest, as they often do in investigations. Then, if the murderer mentioned *this*, it would be obvious they were involved. That is, of course, assuming the authorities simply just didn't mention it. Except that it's *huge*.

Either multiple people are involved in a coverup—including the cops—or nobody thought it was important.

But I spoke to both of Caroline's best friends, and neither of them said anything about this. Is it possible they don't know?

I step into the baby nursery and take it all in. The brightly colored decorations, the happy jungle animals painted on the walls, the crib, the diaper changing table.

Shane and Caroline were clearly expecting a baby. She was pregnant when killed.

This can't be true, can it? Surely, someone would've mentioned it. Especially since Caroline was killed in here. Was the murderer trying to send a message by killing her here? Or did she happen to be here at the time and the nursery was happenstance?

My mind spins with the possibilities. If this happened during the day, Shane could've been at work. If he was in the habit of coming home for lunch, did he walk into the middle of it? He would've tried to fight off the killer. He could've been taken by the assailant.

Or the other, more obvious scenario is that he killed his wife—the statistics are definitely in favor of that theory. There are two times in a woman's life where she's in the most danger. One—when she's pregnant. Two—when she leaves an abusive relationship.

Caroline fit one of those scenarios. Possibly both. If this room indicates what it appears to, she was pregnant. No one would buy all of this stuff before actually conceiving.

But who am I to say? I've never made it that far in any relationship. Also, if what Mia said was true, then Caroline was trying to leave the marriage.

Not that I'm putting much stock into my friend's word right now. How could she think so little of me that she'd been afraid to tell me she made another close friend? That said friend had not only died, but been murdered? That she wanted me to live in her house and solve the murder?

Not only was I being lied to by my boyfriend, but my best friend too. Ian kept stringing me along, saying he wanted marriage and kids, when really he was seeing who knows how many people behind my back. It was no secret that women fell all over him wherever he went—I dealt with people flirting with him right in front of me all the time—though I was dumb enough to believe he was faithful despite the attention.

But I thought I could at least trust my best friend. I poured my heart out to her at least weekly, often more than that. And all the while she was hiding a friendship from me.

Does *anyone* tell the truth anymore?

Guilt stings. I'm standing in a room where a woman and her unborn baby were murdered, and I'm feeling sorry for myself because my ex-boyfriend and best friend lied to me.

Time for some perspective.

I wander the room. Unlike the rest of the house, this one hardly has anything out of place. Anything related to the killing was likely taken as evidence. The folded baby clothes and stacked diapers were probably of no interest to the crime scene investigators.

There's no dried blood or any other indication of how Caroline's life was taken—that was another detail left out of the online reports. I don't even know *how* she died. If she bled out, that was cleaned up by a crew hired by the bank or the agent selling the house.

Why hasn't there been more reported about this murder? It's potentially *two* killings, and even if only one, that means Shane could be out there somewhere alive and in need of help. If kidnapped, he could have been tortured all this time while also mourning the loss of his wife and unborn baby.

It's almost too painful to even think about. Meanwhile, it seems almost everyone thinks he's the perpetrator.

If he's innocent, he needs someone to take his side.

When I do my podcast, I need to go with the unpopular opinion that he's innocent. If he is alive somewhere in hiding and catches wind of my investigation, it could be what he needs to come forward. We all need to hear his side.

Who better to do that than me? I have all the time in the

world to go through his things. If there's evidence the police missed, it would be here in this house—my house.

I'm so glad I have this mystery to distract me from everything else in my life. With any luck, I can find a killer and a missing man.

Maybe even answer the questions about my sister's death, too.

Moving here might have been the best decision I've ever made. I could almost thank Ian for stringing me along. Otherwise, I might not have seen my need to come here.

Zorro comes in. He sniffs the floor, his tail straight up instead of wagging.

Curious, I watch him.

He goes straight toward the crib and stops in front of it, focused on one spot.

"What is it, boy?"

Zorro pays me no attention and continues smelling that particular area. He even sits and paws at the floor.

Could that be where Caroline died?

16

Caroline

Before

It's been a long day, and while my husband and I aren't on the best of terms, I'm actually looking forward to sitting down and having a meal with him—even though I have to cook. As always.

My phone alerts me of a text.

> SHANE
>
> Working late again and getting takeout for dinner.

Before we married, I knew his work as an attorney would keep him busy, but I had no idea just *how* busy he would be with all of the cases. He could work round the clock and still not do enough for his rotating list of clients.

I send a message saying I understand, because I do. Doesn't mean I like it.

Now what am I supposed to do? Warm up leftovers again?

At least I hadn't started cooking anything yet. I hate making food only for myself.

My hand immediately goes to my stomach. Technically, I'm eating for two, but it doesn't feel like it. I've only begun to feel movements—and if I'm being honest, it feels more like gas bubbles than a baby—yet according to online wisdom, that's what it is. I'm also not showing yet. Sure, my clothes are tighter, but again, it's more like bloat than my sweet child. I still don't need my new maternity clothes.

I dig through the fridge, looking for something to warm up. The only real noticeable sign that I'm actually expecting is my food aversions. So far, no nausea or vomiting.

Maybe I should get a cat for company. Shane doesn't like the idea of pets in the house, but it isn't like he's here enough to really care. As long as there aren't animals running around his office, he should be fine. A couple of my foster homes had cats, and I bonded with them in ways I never did with people.

Another text comes in. Maybe Shane is coming home early after all.

It isn't my husband.

SAVANNAH

Want to meet for dinner? My treat!

My heart flutters at the message. I send a quick reply.

CAROLINE

In public? Are you sure? Seems risky.

My phone rings. It's him, even though the name attached to his number shows 'Savannah.'

I accept the call. "Hello, Savannah."

"Hey, Mitch," he replies. It's our running joke, but it's worked so far. Nobody—not even Shane—has suspected calls or messages from Savannah or Mitch.

"Are you serious about going out for dinner?"

"I wish. Sorry to get your hopes up, but I meant our usual."

My heart sinks. I should've known he didn't mean going out for a date. Too risky—not that anything we do is without its own inherent dangers. "Right. Obviously."

"Unless you're ready to leave?" A lot of hope hinges in his voice.

"Not yet. There are too many loose threads." Not the least of which is the fact that I'm trying to leave a lawyer. He knows practically every single other attorney in our county.

I don't stand a chance in court. I'll lose everything.

"Our usual spot?" he asks. "About half an hour. That gives me time to pick up the food and meet you there."

"Reservation under Mitch?"

"As always."

"I'll be there."

"Can't wait." He makes a kissing sound before ending the call.

At least I won't be alone tonight.

Would Shane feel differently about all of his late nights if he knew he was sending me into the arms of another man?

Sometimes it's hard to believe things ever came to this. When we first met, Shane was my rescuer. I was so lonely from years in the foster care system, and I didn't have an education to fall back on. The only jobs I've ever had were minimum wage with long hours.

I finally got adopted in high school, but honestly I'm not sure it was better than aging out of foster care. My family is deeply religious—not something I grew up with at all—and at first I liked a lot of aspects of it. The huge, welcoming extended family. As often as we attended church events, it was like having a ton of aunts, uncles, cousins, and grandparents.

Every foster kid's dream.

But then came the rules. Most of them crushing. As a woman, nobody believed I should go to college. My only value in their eyes was to become a wife and mother. Secondary school would be a waste of my adoptive parents' money and my time.

I needed to learn homemaking skills, and more importantly, my place. So, while my friends from school went off to this university and that, I helped my new mother with laundry, dishes, dusting, and every other kind of cleaning imaginable.

Shane and I were seeing each other secretly, but then one day someone from the church saw us together and told my parents. They freaked out and insisted on meeting him right away. It was a horrifying, humiliating experience, but my boyfriend handled it with ease and won them over almost immediately.

The only problem was, in the Beacon of Truth Fellowship, dating is practically marriage. If you get involved with someone romantically, there's no going back. Even without vows, it's like giving vows. You give your heart, it's game over. That's your partner for life.

Shane joined the church, and we got married almost before I knew what happened. To call it a whirlwind would be the understatement of the century. Our plan was leaving the group after the wedding and honeymoon that my parents paid for fully.

But that wasn't how things played out. Shane soon found how much he enjoyed the role of head of house.

My phone alerts me to another text from 'Savannah' and pulls me from my thoughts. He tells me the hotel reservation is set and I can show up anytime.

I press my palm on my belly. "Time to see your daddy."

17

Fleur

Monday, early evening

Shane's office is a disaster. I've emptied every desk drawer, pulled each book from the shelves and fanned out the pages, and taken everything from the closet. There isn't a nook or cranny I haven't investigated.

If he hid anything, it isn't here. Either he took his secrets with him when he fled the house, or the police have the evidence and haven't returned it. Why would they? It isn't like he's around for them to give anything back to him. The new owner of his house doesn't have any rights to it.

The only thing I've learned is that he was a successful personal injury attorney who often went after huge corporations to fleece them for his clients who paid him massive sums of money for his efforts. Any secrets he has are probably locked away in his office at work.

Nobody would let me in there.

I still have plenty of places to check in the house. His and

Caroline's bedroom still gives me the creeps, but I'm going to have to get over that. That's where any of their secrets are likely to be. Where do I hide diaries and valuables? In my bedroom. Though if I had an office, that would be right up there.

Zorro comes into the room and whines.

A glance at the time tells me I've missed his dinnertime by more than an hour. The sun is already starting to go down outside.

I scratch his ear. "Sorry, boy. Let's get you fed."

He races out of the room, tail wagging.

Just as I'm filling his bowl, the doorbell rings.

Am I expecting someone? I check the peephole.

Darby stands there with a tall, handsome man. Must be her husband. What was his name? Toby? Tony? Something like that. I forgot they were going to come and take the bed from my hands.

I whip open the door. "Hi! Where are your girls?"

"With our next-door neighbor." Darby hands me a casserole dish and introduces me to Troy.

Right. Troy. I'll have to remember that next time.

We shake hands, and he nods his head rather than giving a verbal greeting. "Which way to the bedroom?"

"Darby can show you. I'll put this in the kitchen."

They head down the hallway while I make my way to the oven and put my dinner inside, setting the temperature to a low setting. My stomach growls, and my mouth waters at the aroma.

I hurry to the bedroom, Zorro at my heels. If we're going to get anything accomplished, I need to put him somewhere else. Luckily, he's happy to run into the backyard.

"You sure you want to give this away?" Troy asks when I return, not taking his gaze from the bed. "It looks like it costs a fortune."

"I'm sure. I'd like to get a new bed."

He nods, still not looking at me. Then he grabs the mattress then lugs it out of the room on his own. He must be stronger than he looks.

Darby glances at me. "I think we can get the frame."

It takes some maneuvering to separate the massive headboard, but once we do, we easily move the frame together.

Outside, Troy is loading the mattress into the back of a large pickup truck. He helps Darby and me with the frame, then it takes all three of us to get the headboard loaded. I've broken into a sweat and am gasping for air like I've just run a marathon.

Clearly I need to get back into a workout routine.

Darby gives me a wide smile. "We can't thank you enough for this. You sure we can't pay you?"

"No. Like I said, you're doing me a favor. Plus, you're feeding me. You don't know how much that helps me."

"Glad we can help each other out. Right, Troy?"

He nods again.

Not a talkative guy. Which is fine, because he isn't the one I want to talk to. I have questions about Darby's friendship with Caroline, but that'll have to wait. My stomach is going to eat itself if I don't dig into that casserole soon.

"Maybe I can come over soon?" I say. "I'd love to see your house and meet your girls."

Troy scowls, doesn't even bother to hide his disgust.

Did I do something to offend him?

Darby's expression lights up. "I'd love that!"

"Don't you have that thing tomorrow?" Troy asks.

"Thing?" She throws him a questioning glance.

"Yeah. You know, with the kids."

Darby looks deep in thought for a moment. "You mean story time at the library?"

"Exactly, and they have gymnastics."

"I can still have coffee with Fleur."

He grumbles something, gets into the truck, and roars the engine to life.

"I get the feeling he doesn't like me."

"Don't take it personally."

"That he doesn't like me?"

"It isn't that." She gives me a bright smile. "He gets nervous around new people, that's all. Once he warms up, you'll love him. Troy's just a bit of an acquired taste."

"I'll take your word on that."

Beep!

Darby jumps at the truck's horn blaring. "Guess I'd better get going. Thanks for the bed!"

"And thank you for the meal."

"Come over any time." She waves before running into the vehicle.

The tires peel as they drive away.

It's hard to imagine liking that guy, but maybe he is just shy.

My stomach roars again, and I hurry in and scarf down almost half the casserole in one sitting.

Definitely need to get back into a workout routine.

Zorro scratches at the door, and I let him in after covering the dish. My mind is spinning, and I wish I had someone to talk with about everything I've been learning. Normally that person would be Mia, but she went to such great lengths to hide her friendship with Caroline from me—not only when she was alive, but also when talking me into buying her house.

I don't care that she has other friends. I'm glad and wouldn't want or expect anything else. But it bothers me that she felt the need to hide it from me. Either she thought I was so weak I couldn't handle it, or she had some other reason.

Did she really think I wouldn't find out, especially after moving into this house?

This hurts more than any romantic betrayal. Mia and I have been best friends for half my life. I met her right after Lourdes disappeared, and she helped fill that new void in my life. She knows all of my pains—so she should know how this would affect me.

Yet she did it, anyway.

What I need is some fresh air. And a bed. Definitely a bed. I don't know how many more nights I can deal with sleeping on the couch.

I call Zorro over to the front door, then we go outside. It's nearly dark now, but I don't care. If I have to spend another moment inside the house, I'm going to lose my mind.

There's a bench against the house, and I sit on it. Zorro jumps up and curls next to me. I pat him, and my mind darts from one thought to another—Mia, Caroline, Darby, Lourdes's necklace, the nursery, the bedroom. I can't do anything about most of it, but I can research beds.

I pull out my phone and quickly narrow down my search. Most people would want to test a mattress before purchasing—Ian definitely would—but I don't have to run my decisions past anyone. All I want is a new bed as soon as possible. All of the stores have a trial period, so if I don't like what I pick, I can always try a new one.

Ten minutes later, I've made my decision and ordered the bed. It will be here tomorrow. Ian would've balked at the fee I paid for the faster delivery, but I don't care. It's worth it to me, and that's all that matters.

Zorro sits up, his ears perking.

I follow his gaze to the end of the driveway.

Is that Emmett?

Groaning, I rise. I should've gone into the backyard instead of the front. Too late now.

Emmett waves. "Hey, neighbor. How are you settling in?"

I may as well talk to him. He's one of the few people who will actually give me the time of day. "Not bad. How are you?"

"Great, actually." He beams, not saying more.

Apparently I'm supposed to ask. "Why's that?"

"I just got an amazing role today."

"Role?"

"Hired for a commercial that will play all over the country."

"Wow, that's great."

He looks a little disappointed that I'm not more excited. "It's huge, but I guess you don't know much about the entertainment industry."

"Not that aspect of it."

"Trust me, this is big."

"Congratulations."

"Thanks." He leans against my van.

I should be annoyed by that, but I don't care. As soon as I get around to it, I'm going to trade it in for a cuter car that suits me better than this soccer mom mobile.

"So, you're getting rid of the Porters' things?"

"Pardon?"

"I saw the Wilsons drive off with a bed."

"You don't miss anything, do you?"

"Not that. Looking to lose anything else? I'd be happy to help."

"I'm fine, thanks."

"Caroline and I were friends. She'd be happy for me to have some of her things."

"You were friends only with her? Not Shane?"

He shifts nervously. "Well, he worked a lot. Caroline and I naturally found ourselves talking when I would go on my daily walks."

"Kind of like this?" I take a step back.

"Do I make you nervous?" He steps away from the van, giving me an inquisitive expression.

"No." I'm not sure whether that's the truth, but I'm not going to let him think he's getting to me.

"I'm just trying to be friendly. We're the only singles in this neighborhood. Seems like we should stick together, you know?"

"Singles?"

"Everyone else is either paired up with a partner and kids or a roommate. Not us. We're alone in our big empty houses."

Bumps prickle my arms. "I'm not alone. I have Zorro."

"You know what I mean."

I start to tell him that I'm going inside, but a car pulls up to the curb and parks.

What now?

Mia climbs out of the car, sets her alarm, and waves. "Fleur! I'm so glad I caught you."

I return the wave, even though she's the last person I want to see. But if it'll get Emmett out of my hair, I'll invite her inside. I turn to Emmett. "That's my friend. I'll see you later."

He stiffens. "Yeah, sure. You have my number. Let me know if you need anything."

"I'll do that."

Emmett doesn't look like he believes it any more than I do, but he walks off in the opposite direction as Mia.

"Who's that?" she asks.

"Just a neighbor. I'll see you around."

She frowns. "Please hear me out."

"Why?" I cross my arms. "You've made it clear how little you think of me."

"Let me explain. If you're still mad at me, I'll go and never come back."

As much as I hate the thought of talking with her, I hate the thought of never seeing her again even more.

"Come inside."

18

Fleur

Monday, early evening

Mia and I sit at the couch with glasses of tap water, since that's the only thing I have on hand. Tomorrow I really need to do some proper grocery shopping.

Finally, I can't take the silence any longer. "Why are you here?"

She sighs. "I owe you an apology."

"You think?"

"I should've told you about Caroline."

"Why didn't you?" I ask. "Did you think I was too weak to handle the truth?"

"Never. You're one of the strongest people I know."

I snort. "Right."

"You *are*. Not only did you deal with the loss of your sister, but you had to put up with your parents falling apart after that. You practically raised *them*."

"Then why keep your friendship with Caroline secret?"

She plays with a loose thread on the couch. "At first, it was because we were barely acquaintances. Just seeing each other as we hung out with mutual friends. Then we started spending time together just the two of us. It still wasn't a big deal. But then we started connecting."

"This is starting to sound like an affair. Wait. You didn't—?"

"No! It's nothing like that. We were just friends."

"Best friends."

Mia nods and avoids my eye contact, looks away.

"You still could've brought her up at any time."

"I thought about it."

"Why didn't you?"

She continues playing with that blasted thread before finally meeting my gaze. "Because I didn't want to hurt your feelings! You've always been so fragile, and I knew things were rocky with Ian. You've always leaned on me as your support. I couldn't do that to you."

"I thought you said I'm the strongest person you know."

"Yes."

"How can I be both strong and fragile?"

"Yin and yang. You're two sides of a coin. People are complicated, and you're no different."

"You're giving me a headache." I rub my temples.

She reaches out and takes my hand in hers. "Fleur, you're strong because you have to be. But what you've been through has also broken you in ways you don't talk about. I see it, and I'm glad to be the person you rely on. You *need* someone to be a steady force in your life."

I blink a few times as I stare at her. "You think you're my savior?"

"That isn't what I said."

"Actually, it kind of is."

Silence settles between us.

I speak first. "You make our relationship sound codependent."

"That's not what I meant."

"It's what you're describing."

Mia sighs loudly. "Look, I messed up, and I'm sorry. I shouldn't have hidden my friendship with Caroline from you. By the time I realized how close we'd grown, I didn't know how to tell you without hurting your feelings. It seemed like it didn't matter, because you were all the way in New York. Then"—her voice cracks—"Caroline died. It was pointless to bring her up then."

"Pointless?" I balk. "Your best friend died, and you didn't even tell me! I didn't even have the opportunity to be there for you. You didn't give me that chance."

Tears shine in her eyes. "I know. But I got through it."

"Without me."

"No. When we talked, it really helped me."

I pull my hand from hers. "This is unbelievable. You were hurting in the worst way, and you hid it from me."

"It was for the best. You were struggling with Ian. The last thing you needed was more on your plate."

"Are we even friends?"

"Of course. You're my best friend."

"Now that Caroline is gone."

"I have enough room in my heart for two best friends."

"How can you say I'm your best friend? You wouldn't even lean on me when you were hurting over such a monumental loss."

She frowns. "I did. You just didn't know it."

"This is too much to process right now. I need you to leave."

Tears fall from her eyes. "This isn't going to ruin our friendship, is it?"

A lump forms in my throat. "I don't know."

"Nothing has to change."

"Everything already has, Mia."

Her shoulders slump, and a look of defeat covers her face. "I understand."

I wait for her to leave, and she finally walks toward the door.

A thought strikes me, and I stop her.

"Do you know what's in the murder room?" I ask.

"What do you mean?"

"Have you been in there?"

She covers her mouth for a moment. "I can't even look in there. I'm the one who locked it in the first place. I probably should have told you that too."

"Probably. But do you know what the room was used for?"

"It was her craft room. Caroline made all the curtains and blankets in this house. She was the most creative person I've ever met."

Interesting. Mia doesn't know about the nursery—unless she's lying about that too.

She tilts her head. "Why do you ask? Have you gone in there?"

"Do you know if she and Shane planned on having kids?"

Her brows draw together. "Caroline wanted a baby more than anything, but Shane was so busy with work, any attempts were futile. She thought maybe he didn't want to have kids. It was a strong point of contention between them."

I study her but don't see any signs of deception.

Apparently Mia wasn't the only one keeping secrets from her best friend.

Had Caroline told anyone she was pregnant? Or was the nursery her own longing for a baby? Kind of like how some people live as if their dream was a reality in order to try and manifest it?

The mystery deepens. I'm going to do my own digging before trying to figure out what Mia really knows.

"Thanks for telling me all you know." I open the door and motion for her to leave. "Don't worry, I'll do everything I can to figure out what really happened."

She steps outside. "I appreciate it. I'm sorry I didn't tell you the truth about why I wanted you to move here."

"The important thing is now I know I can't trust anything you say."

Her mouth falls open. "I suppose I deserve that."

I don't disagree.

"Know that I really am sorry. I hope you can forgive me."

"I hope so too. I'd hate to lose a friendship I've had for half my life. How long has it been based on a lie?"

She doesn't respond.

"How long were you two friends before she died?"

"Two years."

"A total of four years that you kept this from me."

Mia sighs. "Our *friendship* isn't a lie. Everything else is genuine."

"But one lie taints everything else—especially a big one like this."

She turns toward the driveway. "Call me when you're ready to talk. I'll be waiting."

"Okay."

Mia waits a moment before shuffling toward her car.

I close and lock the door, sink onto the couch, then release my tears. It isn't the fact that she made a new best friend that hurts so much, it's that she hid it from me for so long. Was she planning on hiding it forever? Did she really think I could move here and solve the murder mystery without ever finding out she was friends with Caroline?

The whole thing is messed up, especially considering Mia doesn't seem to know anything about the nursery. How long before she died did Caroline change the room from a craft room to a nursery? Was she planning on telling Mia?

Maybe there's a clue in the room itself. If Caroline was pregnant, surely there would be an ultrasound image or something in there indicating an actual pregnancy. I can't imagine anyone going to so much effort to decorate that room if they weren't actually expecting.

I blow my nose then head for the nursery. If the answers aren't there, they must be somewhere in this house.

It's only a matter of time before I find them.

19

The Watcher

Hiding in safety

This is so ridiculous. Beyond ridiculous, really. I'm the one who orchestrated Fleur returning to town and buying that house. Now I can't get near her. She's already back to Miss Popularity and her home is Grand Central Station with a revolving door of guests.

I can't get her alone.

Deep breaths. I take several.

They don't help. What a crock. Why do people always say that when someone gets stressed? Fixing my problem is what will make me feel better.

What I need is a contingency plan. If I can't get to her, I need to find a way to bring her to me.

That listing agent is more of a problem than I thought. I knew Mia might make things challenging, but I didn't realize to what extent.

If I had something to throw and break, I would. I probably

need to go to the gym and take out my frustrations on something there. A punching bag would be ideal, but those are always taken.

The lights in Fleur's house go black one by one. She must be going to bed.

What I wouldn't give to join her. I've watched her from afar for so long. Nearly followed her across the country.

I'd have captured her attention then! Imagine that—the shock on her face seeing me in New York. If she even recognized me from high school. But the cards never fell into place, so I've been here living a second rate life.

That can change now. Fleur Bardot is back in town. Back in my very neighborhood! She's even unattached, having left behind that loser who didn't deserve her in the first place.

Surely she's looking for love. She has to be. I'll bet her biological clock is ticking like a time bomb. Like every other woman at that age.

I need to jump on that opportunity.

This is finally our time. Our lives are in completely different places than they once were, and now I have the chance to not only capture her attention but show her we're made for each other. I just need to get closer to her to study her. Once I know exactly what she wants, I'll become that.

She won't be able to turn me down.

Unlike in high school when she wouldn't even study with me.

Now things are different.

The only thing that hasn't changed is my feelings for her. No, those are stronger than ever. I could hardly breathe when I was near her. Almost close enough to touch.

My heart nearly explodes out of my chest just thinking about it.

If I can just get her alone for a real conversation, then I can show her I'm the ideal man for her. She won't be able to say no.

I only have to figure out how to make that happen. Show myself to be better than all of the other subpar options out there.

There are certain things every woman finds irresistible, and once I find out what Fleur's are, I'll be in.

Forever.

It's only a matter of making that happen.

I'm going to do that sooner rather than later.

Then all my dreams will come true.

And she won't be able to get away. Not even if she wants to. I'll see to that.

Once I get what I want, I'm never letting go. Unlike those fools she's been with in the past that she has always posted about on social media.

20

Fleur

Tuesday, late morning

Ding-dong!
 I bolt upright, nearly falling off the couch.

The sun shines in the house brightly. It takes me a moment to realize the bed delivery must be here.

Ding-dong!

I didn't set my alarm. How late is it? I scramble to my feet, pulling my hair into a messy bun and calling, "I'm coming!"

This is not the start to my day that I imagined.

Hopefully I don't resemble the disaster that I feel like. No time to check.

I fling open the door.

A lady about my age and a guy at least two decades older in matching uniforms greet me. The man hands me a bright bouquet of sunflowers.

My favorite.

I take them from him. "Thanks?"

"They were against your door."

"Oh." That makes a little more sense. I think. Spinning the flowers around, I don't see a card.

Some kind of welcome to the neighborhood gift? Seems kind of odd given most people are unhappy about my arrival.

The lady clears her throat. "Where do you want the bed?"

Before I can answer, the guy speaks. "If you have a mattress to donate, we should take that first."

"I don't have anything. Follow me." I lead them down the hallway.

Items are strewn all around from my searching the house last night.

Heat floods my cheeks. "Sorry I kept you waiting. And about the mess. I just moved in."

"Looks more like you had a rager," the lady says.

I don't know if I'm supposed to give them a tip, but I'm leaning toward not giving her one.

"In there." I point to the bedroom.

"Do you want us to put the frame together?" asks the guy.

"That would be great."

The two of them head back to the front door, and I pick up as many items as I can while still holding the mysterious sunflowers.

I made a bigger mess of this place than the cops likely did, and that's saying something. Once I'm convinced the bed can be safely brought in, I take the bouquet to the kitchen and place it in a vase I find in one of the cabinets.

One of the benefits of this house is that it has literally everything I need. I should feel guilty using a dead woman's things, but I need them, and it isn't like she can come back for them. Hopefully she'd be happy everything is getting use again.

But that doesn't explain whether the sunflowers were intentional. It could've been a coincidence, but those aren't typical fall flowers. Did I tell someone about them? I've had so many conversations since returning, it's hard to remember details like that. It's also been my favorite flower since I was a kid, so someone could remember the fact and hope it's still true.

Either way, I don't know whether this is a *welcome to the neighborhood* gift or an ominous sign—possibly worse than the tires.

Whoever sent these knows what my favorite flower is.

Footsteps sound behind me, pulling me from my thoughts.

The male delivery person says, "The bed is set up. Do you need anything else?"

"Let me have a look before you go." I hurry past them, not giving them a chance to object.

It looks exactly as I pictured. Now I just need to get rid of everything else in this room, but that'll take time. At least I can get a good night's sleep and roll over without smashing my face against the back of a couch.

"What do you think?" asks the lady with an exasperated tone.

"It's perfect. Thank you."

The guy nods. "You have ninety days to return it. The guys at the store might try to talk you out of it, but don't let them. They just don't want to deal with the extra paperwork. If you don't like it for any reason, we'll take it back. But it *has* to be in that time frame, and not a day later."

"Thanks for the tip. I appreciate it."

"Exchanges are no problem. Have a nice day."

"You, too."

They head down the hallway. I follow them, lock the door after they leave, then turn around to face the mess I made last night.

Mess isn't a strong enough word.

My efforts were for nothing. I didn't find any proof of a pregnancy. Chances are, if there were any medical records or ultrasound printouts, the police have them. I might have to go in and talk to a detective.

If what Darby told me is true, they aren't likely to say much. But I need to find out if anyone knew Caroline was expecting. It could be a motive.

I also need to find out if either Mia or Darby knew. Just because they haven't mentioned it, doesn't mean they don't know anything. I'm used to interviewing people who have things to hide, but this case is unlike any other. I'm living in the crime scene.

My missing sister's locket is also somehow involved.

Is someone trying to tell me Lourdes's case somehow intertwined with this one?

Before I start cleaning this mess or trying to solve the mystery, I need food and a shower. Then I have to wash the sheets after being on the floor and put them on the new bed.

It'll feel so good to have a brand new mattress after the couch and the various budget motels I stayed in along the way.

But that's hours away. I have a lot to do today before I try my new bed.

In addition to everything around here, I really need to post an updated podcast. The pleas on my social media and inbox are getting out of control. People are dying of curiosity. Not that I can blame them. It isn't every day a true crime podcaster moves into a murder house to solve a mystery.

As far as I know, I'm the first.

I need to make an episode before my listeners get annoyed or bored and unsubscribe.

My shower and breakfast are going to have to wait.

21

Chasing the Forgotten Ones

Murder House Series: Part 1: Fleur Bardot, podcaster

First, this will be a shorter podcast than normal. It's a quick update as I haven't had much time yet to research the Porter case. Usually when I post episodes, I've already done all the research and have spent time making and editing them. This one is going out as-is so you can catch up quickly. I appreciate your understanding.

Second, thank you for your patience as I've moved across the country with only my adorable sidekick, Zorro, and settled into my new home—the murder house. To be honest, I'm not sure I'll ever feel settled here. Time will tell.

It's strange and most unsettling to live where someone died. As I've explained in episodes 159 and 161, Caroline Porter was found murdered in her home two years ago. Her husband Shane was missing and remains so to this day.

Neither had family who claimed the house or the possessions. Everything the police left remains. So I'm taking this unique opportunity to step into the middle of a missing persons case and unsolved murder by moving in and living where Caroline and Shane lived. Because their belongings are still here, I'm hoping to learn more about them and the crime than I typically manage during my research.

Some have called me crazy and worse. I know this is unconventional, and I deeply appreciate all of you who support me. If this experiment goes as planned, we can solve a murder and missing persons case together.

Maybe we'll even find Shane alive and well. Most think he fled after killing his wife—and the statistics certainly point in that direction—but nobody knows for sure. There are cases of husbands who are innocent in their wives' deaths. It happens, just not often. This could be one of those cases.

I'm going in with an open mind, and I'm assuming him innocent until proven guilty... which brings me to an important point that I want you, dear listeners, to spread far and wide. It may not be popular, but I feel it needs to be done.

If Shane Porter is alive somewhere, I want him to reach out to me. He needs someone to give him a voice, someone to let him share his story. I'll interview him however and wherever he wants. He doesn't have to give up his location—we can talk over video or the phone. It doesn't matter.

I simply want to give him a platform to tell his side of the story. This case has hardly been publicized, and if he's alive, he's a wanted man.

Shane and I went to high school together briefly. If I remember correctly, he was a senior when I was a freshman. From what I knew of him, he had a great reputation, was always kind to others, and I can't recall anyone having a bad thing to say about him even one time.

He may have even been friends with my sister Lourdes, which adds a personal element to this case. I believe you're innocent, Shane. Let me help you.

Somebody needs to get to the bottom of this, and since nobody else has stepped up, that person is me.

Shane, if you reach out to me, your location will remain confidential. You don't have to tell me. I just want to help get your story out there. You deserve to be heard.

Let's lock it in.

Dramatic pause.

Now, onto the stuff you listeners have been waiting for—what it's been like moving into a murder house.

First, I need clear up one thing. I am not demented or crazy or any of the other colorful names some people have called me. Anyone who has been listening to this podcast for any length of time knows I make these episodes and wrote my book because of one reason.

Bringing the lost home.

It all started because I couldn't let go of the hope that my sister's case would be solved one day. Fifteen years after her disappearance, Lourdes Bardot is still missing, and her case is as cold as a freezer.

It is still my heart's biggest desire to solve that case. In the meantime, I'm throwing myself into other cases such as this one. I love being able to play a part in bringing closure to other families.

Shane and Caroline's case is different in many aspects. One being that they were both foster kids, and though Caroline was adopted, it appears her new family doesn't want to say anything publicly. That's partly why this case fizzled so fast. There aren't any online fund collections or social media groups or pages dedicated to finding her.

Then there's Shane. Literally nobody is looking for him.

He's missing. What if the killer has been holding him hostage this entire time? Nobody is looking for him because he looks guilty.

Listen to me when I say this—we don't know what part, if any, he played in his wife's death.

That's why I want to reach out to him. He needs to know that someone believes he could be innocent. I have to talk to him. How often do we get to hear from the suspects? Usually the best I can provide is a recording of police interviews.

What if I could get a personal interview with him? That would be as unique as my moving into the Porter's house.

Sorry, I got off track again. You want to hear about the house, but my heart is always for the victims and I can't help but talk about them. And to be clear, I'm going to assume that Shane Porter is a victim in this case until I learn otherwise.

Back to the house.

It looks like what you would expect from a home that's been abandoned for two years. It needs a lot of work to become a home again.

Stepping inside was strange, like I was someone's houseguest. It still kind of feels that way, as most of the things in here belonged to them. My only belongings are what I was able to drive here with in the van I purchased.

In other news, if anyone is interested in buying a reliable mini-van, let me know!

I still have a lot to do with the house and the Porter's things, so I'll have more to share in my next episode. In the meantime, check out my social media pages for some pictures I just posted. Comment and share—we might be able to reach Shane.

If you want to see exclusive images, make sure you're part of my private online community. That's where I'm going to share the most exciting details first. Don't worry, everything will be public at some point. But if you can't wait, join there. Supporters are already discussing a myriad of theories. Jump into the conversation!

As always, you can find all links in the show notes.

Until next time, stay safe and hug your loved ones tightly—you never know when one of you might go missing.

22

Caroline

Before

I can't wipe the smile from my face as I pull into my neighborhood. These nights when I can get away from the house are the best I could ask for. Unlike my husband, my baby's dad makes me feel like the most special person in the world, like I'm a queen and a world-class award winner all wrapped up into one.

He appreciates me in a way Shane hasn't in years. When we were young and both part of the foster care system, we were each other's only cheerleaders. We believed in each other in ways nobody else did. Nobody else we knew could understand us—they all had natural families who supported them.

Now Shane has his law firm, and that fills all of his needs. He gets praise, adoration, accolades, money. What does he need from me?

Nothing.

If I didn't have this new relationship, that thought would

kill me. But now I too have someone who showers me with what I need, and in return I give him all the same.

My grin fades as I near the house.

Shane's car is out front.

My stomach sinks so far, it goes through the car floor and onto the street below.

He's going to be furious. I didn't tell him I was leaving, and he hates it when I do that—even though I never know where he's going. But that type of a double standard is acceptable in our circles.

Our church teaches that men are the rulers at home, and whatever they say goes.

I could turn around and not come home tonight. Then I won't have to deal with Shane's anger or accusations.

But that'll only last a night. Eventually, I'll have to face the music.

If I don't go along with Shane's wishes, he can take me to the Beacon of Truth Fellowship council. They'll make my life even more miserable than whatever my husband unleashes on me at home.

No, I have to go home and face him. I just need to think of something believable.

I slow as I get closer to the driveway. Glance in the back seat for anything I can say I was shopping for, but there isn't anything new there.

Maybe I can tell him it's a surprise. It's still a little ways off until his birthday, but he might buy it. I do love planning parties. We haven't even told anyone about our baby, and I already have the shower completely figured out. It's believable.

I hope.

My heart hammers as I pull into the driveway, parking next to Shane's much nicer sedan. He works, so he gets the better vehicle. Can't argue that logic. Well, I *could*, but it wouldn't do me any favors.

Part of the blinds lift in the living room.

He's waiting for me.

My hands shake as I reach for my purse. It takes three tries to pick it up.

I sniff my hair, making sure it doesn't smell like cologne. There's no mistaking the two. Shane's is a strong scent expected from a man who thinks he's all powerful. The one that's probably clinging to me is a more woodsy, rugged variety.

Just the thought of it makes my insides melt.

If I think about *him* while I talk to Shane, I should be able to stand my ground. Not give in and admit I've done wrong.

How is what I've done any worse than what Shane has done? I've smelled several different kinds of perfume on him over the last year.

Not that the church will see it my way. My husband is the leader of the home, so he can do what he wants. I'll be scolded for not going along with him and staying faithful. Apparently wives are nothing more than dogs to this group.

That's why I'm trying to get out of the Beacon of Truth Fellowship. It won't be easy. I've signed a very scary membership agreement with an even more frightening NDA.

Worse, over the years several unhappy wives mysteriously vanished, never to be spoken of again. We don't talk about outsiders, and especially not those who walked away, breaking their membership vows.

The vows to the church are way more intense than any wedding promises.

The front door opens. Shane stands in the doorway.

I'm taking too long to get inside.

He motions me over.

I give him a friendly wave, like I can't wait to see him.

Not that he's going to buy it.

Think, think!

My mind won't cooperate. It's too much pressure. I'm going

to fold. He's going to know the truth. The fact that he was cheating first won't matter. I'm not supposed to cheat at all, ever, for any reason.

Double standards are an oppressive force in my pitiful existence. I wish I'd never met my last foster family, that they'd never adopted me and brought me into this community. It was all for show, to make them look good for helping an orphan. They married me off as soon as possible, once Shane joined the group.

A lump forms in my throat as I step out of the car and lock it.

I need to forget about my beautiful house and the nursery I've already decorated and stocked.

The only thing that matters is my baby and his or her daddy. If we can run away together, we won't have to deal with any of this. I can forget all about Shane and our terrible friends. But in this town? Not one person will stand up for me, not given what I've done.

My hand instinctively goes to my stomach as I take slow, measured steps toward the door.

Shane doesn't step closer to me. Whatever he has to say to me, he wants to say it in the privacy of our own home.

That's what scares me the most.

He's staring me down, not taking his gaze from me.

My expression has to give away my fear, I'm sure of it. Tears sting my eyes.

I never should've left that hotel room. Leaving behind everything I own would be worth it. The Beacon of Truth Fellowship says it all belongs to Shane anyway, since he's the head of the household.

He doesn't budge when I reach the porch.

My blood runs cold. What does he have planned?

"Where were you?" Shane's expression is hard to read—he could be curious or furious. I can't tell which.

I swallow. "I just wanted some air. If I knew you'd be coming home this soon, I'd have made sure to get back earlier. You could've called me."

"I tried."

I still can't read him. That makes it harder to know how to react. I struggle to find the words.

"Where were you?" he repeats.

Something deep within me tells me to run.

I do. As I spin around, I remote-unlock the door and jump inside as fast as I can.

He races after me, pleading. "Talk to me, Caroline!"

"I can't do this!" Fumbling, I slam the car door shut. Slide the key in the ignition and start the engine. Pull into the street without looking. Squeal the tires. Burn rubber as I make my way back out of the neighborhood.

Hot tears fall onto my cheeks as I struggle with my seatbelt, somehow managing to get it locked into place.

I head for the only place I can go—the hotel. Though my boyfriend checked out, he did pay for the night. With any luck, I can get back in.

Shane will never forgive me when he finds out the truth about the baby. There's no way I'm going to risk church discipline. They could take away my child. Lock me up and never let me see daylight or my loved ones again.

I can't trust anyone, and not even my husband. Given what I found in his office the other day, there's no denying I'm not safe with him. I was so shocked, I stuffed it in the back of a drawer near the top. He won't be able to find it again unless he knows exactly where it is.

He won't be able to get rid of the proof now.

I may have been able to convince myself he was fine before, but not anymore. He's hiding a terrifying secret about Lourdes Bardot. It scares me to my core.

23

Fleur

Wednesday, late morning

This bed is so comfortable, I don't think I ever want to climb out. I'm definitely not returning it—it's the perfect softness and is a million times better than the couch. I'm also still exhausted from yesterday. After putting my bedding on the mattress, I spent the entire rest of the day picking up the messes around the house.

I almost finished the job, except I still have Shane's office to go through. But that will have to wait.

Assuming I get out of bed, I need to check my social media and private community forum. After I published my podcast episode, comments everywhere blew up. Usually I have a hard time keeping up on a normal day, but if things keep going at this rate, I'll have to hire someone just to field comments.

Thinking about all I have to do, I pull myself out of bed and head into the hallway. I stop outside the messy office. I really should clean it up. It's disappointing that I didn't find anything in there. I really thought there would be *something* tucked away that would give me a clue as to where Shane might be.

If he's hiding something, it isn't in here. I'm going to have to keep looking. There might be something in the garage—or even hidden in a more secretive spot, like tucked under a floorboard.

I'm not going to give up until I find something.

In the meantime, I do need to put things away. Then once that's done, I can figure out my next steps—there are neighbors to speak with, work colleagues, cops, church friends. I have no shortage of leads.

Moving into their house, I really thought I'd find more, get a better picture of their lives behind closed doors. But I'm not sure what I thought I'd find that the police didn't already seize and go through themselves. In fact, they likely still have anything telling in boxes somewhere.

Not that it'll stop me from exploring. One small thing could crack the case wide open, and I'm the right person to find it— even if it's a year down the road.

I start moving things from the floor back to his desk and shelves, my mind busy with my to-do list.

When I pull open an emptied drawer, a paper shifts in the very back. I more sense it than see it. Initially, I think it's a figment of my imagination.

But it can't be.

I reach my arm all the way in, not wanting to pull the drawer any farther and risk squishing whatever just fell loose. It takes some finagling, but finally my fingertips contact the paper.

It isn't just any paper. It feels like a photo.

Why would Shane hide a photo way back here?

It must be important—something worth hiding.

My breath hitches as I struggle to pull the picture loose without harming it. It takes some serious stretching and twisting, but I manage to get it free. The top of the drawer scratches my skin as I pull my arm out.

Then I sit back and shake off the photo.

What I see makes my heart skip a beat before exploding in my chest. My mouth falls open as I stare at it.

I have to be imagining this.

But I'm not. The photo falls from my fingers and floats to the floor. I pick it back up with shaky hands and take in the image.

I'm holding a picture of a very young Shane kissing my sister. There's no doubt that's Lourdes on the other side of Shane's lips.

Why does he have this? I don't understand. He was married to Caroline, so why keep this picture after all that time?

I don't know what to do with this.

Especially after finding the locket outside.

These two cases are undeniably linked. Now I want to talk to Shane more than ever—there has to be a reason he hung onto this photo all this time.

Lourdes has been missing for fifteen years, and I'm certain this picture was taken not long before that. I recognize her yellow shirt. She'd been so proud of it because it looked like one her favorite actress wore in a recent movie.

It was also the shirt she wore in so many of the missing posters that ended up plastered all over town. That shirt practically became synonymous with my sister. People all around the world saw it. The picture was shared all over social media, and numerous posts went viral.

I hate to say it, but she would've loved knowing she got more attention wearing that shirt than the celebrity she adored.

However, the shirt isn't what's important here. It's her lips locked with Shane Porter days, or even hours, before her disappearance.

My stomach churns acid. He was involved with Lourdes around the time she disappeared.

Tears sting my eyes. This can't be. But I can't deny photographic evidence. Images couldn't have been altered so easily back then. Sure, it was possible with more rudimentary versions of editing software, but not in the ways it is now.

The longer I stare at the picture, the worse I feel. In fact, my stomach lurches.

I drop the photo and run to the bathroom. Make it to the toilet just in time. I'm glad I hadn't eaten anything yet this morning, or I'd lose even more food.

I'm not sure I'll be able to eat *anything* today now.

After brushing my teeth, I make my way down the hall with trembling legs.

Shane, who is suspected of murdering his wife, was making out with my sister before *she* disappeared.

Lourdes and Shane were together when she disappeared.

Everything is suddenly far more complicated than I thought.

Someone else must know, because there's no other explanation for the locket being in the backyard the other night.

A lump forms in my throat, and tears blur my vision.

This cannot be happening.

But it is.

24

Fleur

Thursday, early afternoon

I really should get out of bed. I've been in here for more than a day, and still haven't eaten anything—unless you count cookies and ice cream. Somehow I've managed to keep that down, despite hardly being able to process that photo of my sister and Shane.

How could they have been playing tonsil hockey the same time she disappeared? She'd been keeping more secrets from me than I thought. And here I believed I'd uncovered them all.

I'll likely never know all of Lourdes's secrets. She took most of them to the grave, as evidenced by the picture of her and Shane. They were really going at it too—that wasn't some casual kiss. And who was behind the camera? Someone took it.

That means *the photographer* knows about the relationship. Maybe they're the one who left me the locket to find.

But why?

I need to know more. Were Shane and Lourdes actually

seeing each other when she disappeared? Could that picture have been some kind of joke or a dare? Since I don't know who took the photo, it's impossible to say.

Knowing my sister, I wouldn't put it past her to have staged the scene to make someone jealous or to get something she wanted from another person. That was how she rolled, not that anyone talked about her machinations after she went missing.

Once gone, she was the perfect all-American girl who could do no wrong. Except everyone at school knew the truth—me more than most since I lived with her. I saw her going out with a different guy every night, even boys with girlfriends.

She didn't care. What she wanted, she got.

Until it all came back to catch up with her. Someone she took advantage of or stabbed in the back is behind her disappearance. They made her pay for everything.

But who? Could it have been Shane? Despite how damning the picture seems, he was only one guy in a line of many. Lourdes could've kissed half a dozen other guys that same day.

Except there aren't any pictures of that. Only the one hidden away in Shane's office desk.

I need real food, and I need to get out of this house to find answers. People in the neighborhood knew the adult Shane.

It's time to find out how he changed since high school. Since making out with my sister.

Acid churns in my stomach again. I really need to stop thinking about that picture. Chances are, it doesn't mean anything. Ninety percent of the guys in our high school likely have similar photos. Any of them could have killed her. What are the odds Shane had anything to do with it? Pretty low, given how many people Lourdes dissed over the years.

That's why the chances of her case being solved are so low.

Too many suspects. It could honestly be *anyone*. Maybe even somebody who didn't go to our school. It could've been another cheerleader from a competing school, or even a teacher or one of their wives. She had multiple affairs, though now it would be called abuse by the teachers.

I need to get Lourdes off my mind and focus on Caroline. If I'm going to post another podcast episode soon, I have to stay on target. I'm certainly not going to mention the picture. Not unless I find actual proof that he might've done something to my sister. At this point, he's just another tongue in her mouth.

Somehow I find the energy to push off the covers, gather the empty ice cream bowls, and make my way to the kitchen. The sink is in front of me, yet all I can see is the picture of Shane and my sister making out.

If only I hadn't found that. Now it's going to color how I see everything else.

I can't see him as guilty. I've already made it clear that I'm going into this assuming Shane is innocent—that's how I'll draw him out. A chat with him would be the interview of the decade now that I'm drumming up interest in this case.

Since I've started posting about my move here, the number of hits on the case have been growing exponentially. At least I'm doing something. People are talking about the murder, even if only because I'm now living in the house where it took place.

I need to get outside in neutral surroundings, get my sister and Shane off my mind, and get back to the reason I moved here—to find Caroline's killer. Sitting here ruminating is only making it harder for me to stay focused and open minded. Right now Shane looks guilty, and I can't let myself go there.

After grabbing a quick, healthy bite to eat and feeding Zorro, I take the world's fastest shower before heading outside with my pup. Walking him not only gives me an excuse to explore the neighborhood, but he's so cute and friendly, people will have an easier time talking to me—the stranger who moved into the murder house.

Black clouds darken the sky overhead, and I swear thunder rumbles in the distance.

Not surprisingly, there aren't many people outside. Not with a storm looming.

It won't stop me from trying to talk with someone. Zorro and I both have plenty of energy to burn, so if anyone within walking distance is outside, we'll find them.

We go the opposite direction from where Darby and Emmett live. I've already spoken with them. What I need is some new people who can offer fresh perspectives.

I'm about to give up and return home when a woman exits her house.

Her eyes widen as we make eye contact. I'm pretty sure she was one of the people whispering about me that morning I came home from that awful bakery.

I head straight for her, waving and smiling.

She can't ignore me now. Well, she could. But she doesn't. She does stiffen as I stop at the edge of her perfectly manicured lawn—the complete opposite as mine. "Can I help you?"

Some greeting. I ignore her rudeness and introduce myself and Zorro.

The woman nods, an awkward expression on her face. She doesn't come near me or offer a hand.

"Do you have a name?" I ask.

Her gaze darts around before answering. "Sasha."

"So nice to meet you."

If she notices my dripping sarcasm, she doesn't indicate it. "Well, I need to get back inside. Looks like it's going to storm soon."

"Did you know Caroline Porter?" No sense in beating around the bush since she obviously wants to get away from me.

Sasha jolts. "Pardon?"

"I just moved into her house, and it bothers me that her murder hasn't gotten much attention. She deserves to have justice, don't you think?"

"Um… yeah." She glances all around, everywhere but toward me.

"Do I make you nervous?"

She finally turns to me. "What?"

"You don't seem happy to be talking with me."

Her only answer is to take a few steps back.

"How well did you know Caroline? Would you say you were friends?"

Sasha clears her throat. "Like I said, the weather's going to turn soon. I don't want to get caught in the lightning. You should probably get your dog inside."

"Are you inviting me in?"

Color drains from her face. "No! I mean, no. Luke and I don't let animals into our home. You really ought to leave. It could be dangerous out here."

Dangerous. Interesting choice of words. Could she be referring to something other than the weather?

There's only one way to find out.

I need to talk to more of our neighbors. I'm not going to let an impending storm get in my way. It could be another hour before rain starts to fall.

That gives me plenty of time.

25

Fleur

Thursday, early afternoon

By the time I've almost completely circled the neighborhood, I'm thoroughly discouraged. Sasha was the only person outside, though I heard a door slam somewhere, which made me think someone was trying to avoid me. Normally that would sound like an absurd thought, but not here.

Most people seem to want nothing to do with me, and at least one person actively wants me out of here. At least my van tires are still aired up. Hopefully I showed them I won't be held back.

As I approach another house with a lawn in dire need of mowing, the front door opens.

Maybe I'll be able to talk with someone else. Perhaps this walk around the neighborhood wasn't a total waste, after all.

Emmett steps out. His expression lights up and he waves to me.

Him again? I've already spoken to him multiple times. Perhaps I can pick his brain some more. He might know something, and it isn't like anyone else is eager to see me.

He hurries over, kneels down to Zorro's level, and baby talks him while patting his head.

Zorro's tail wags furiously, and he licks Emmett's hand several times.

At least that's a good sign. Dogs are said to be able to sense people's motives.

Emmett rises and gives me a wide smile.

He's just as ridiculously handsome as before.

"I take it this is your house." I gesture toward it.

"Yeah. Technically, my parents'. They spend the cold months down south, and I take care of the place while their gone."

"They don't mind you letting the grass go?"

He chuckles. "I've fallen behind, haven't I?"

"Like I'm one to talk."

"You have a better excuse. My house hasn't been sitting abandoned for two years."

"But I've been here long enough to do something about it."

"I'm sure you have a million things to take care of there. I'll tell you what—when I mow my lawn, I'll come over and take care of yours too. That's one less thing for you to worry about."

"You don't have to do that."

"Obviously, but I'm offering." He shrugs. "But if you don't want me to, I won't."

"Hey, I'm not going to stop you from cutting my grass."

"Great. Just don't expect it too soon. I have several auditions this week, and I'm going to have to spend hours practicing. It's tedious work sometimes."

"I'm sure." I try to think of a way to naturally bring Caroline into the conversation but can't, so I opt for a blunt change in subject. "How well did you know Caroline Porter?"

Emmett tilts his head. "Jumping right into that, are you?"

"You said you don't have much time. I want to solve the mystery."

He sighs. "Good luck with that. The Beacon of Truth Fellowship members are dead set on keeping that under wraps."

"That's weird."

"Right? Almost like they have something to hide."

"Do you think they do?" I study him, having a hard time seeing anything beyond his good looks.

Emmett scratches his chin. "It's hard to say."

"Why's that?"

"They all keep to themselves. It's definitely not an outreach-oriented group, unlike most other churches. The members are pretty exclusive from what I can tell. Everyone seems to think they're better than outsiders. If you ask me, they'd do *anything* to protect their own."

"Anything?"

He nods. "Good luck getting any information from any of them."

"I don't suppose Sasha is part of the group?"

"Sasha Drake?"

"Tall with bottled red hair and a mole near her eye?"

Emmett chuckles. "That's the one. I'm pretty sure everyone on their cul-de-sac goes there."

That explains her gaze darting from house to house when talking to me.

"I'm guessing she didn't give you the warmest welcome?"

"That would be correct."

He glances at his fitness watch. "I'd love to talk more, but I have an audition to get to. We should talk again soon. Over dinner?"

"Dinner."

"My treat." He gives me a devilish grin. "What do you say?"

"I'll get back to you."

"You already have my number?"

"Right."

"Perfect. Let me know what works for you." He smiles at me again.

He's either the happiest guy alive or he's hiding something.

Emmett makes his way over to a ten-year-old car that could use some new paint.

That reminds me I need to trade in the van for something more my style.

I watch him as he pulls out of the driveway—smiling, of course—and disappears around the corner.

A crack of thunder sounds in the distance. The storm will be here soon, so I should make my way back home. But Darby's house is so close. Other than Emmett, she's the only one in this neighborhood who wants anything to do with me. And as one of Caroline's best friends, she must know something that will help point me in the right direction.

She won't know anything about Shane's connection to Lourdes, but even if she wasn't close with Caroline right before her death, she must know something useful. Even if she doesn't know it. I can help her figure out what might get us somewhere.

More thunder sounds, but it's still far away. I can pop in really quick and make it back home before the pouring rain and lightning makes its way here. Even if I don't, I can handle some rain.

There aren't any cars in front of Darby's house, but they might be one of those families who actually uses the garage for cars and not storage.

I walk up, noting several cameras along the way. Could those have caught anything in regard to Caroline's murder? Or were they installed more recently? As a result of the crime?

Once at the door, I ring the bell even though they have to already know I'm here with all the cameras.

Pattering of feet and squeals of laughter sound inside before a very frazzled Darby answers the door. "Fleur! What a surprise. How are you doing?"

Two small girls run behind her, laughing and chasing a German shepherd who has a ribbon on its tail.

Zorro whines and inches toward the door.

I tug on his leash, indicating for him to stay put. "I'm fine. I was hoping we could talk. Is this a bad time?"

Darby tucks some hair behind an ear. "Lunchtime is always hectic around here."

The dog and girls circle back around, this time the older daughter has something bright pink spread across her face and the other one holds a thick felt marker.

Zorro wiggles, tugging on his leash. Obviously he wants to get in on the fun too.

I pat his head while keeping a tight grip on the leash. "I could come back later."

"I'd love that. Emma and Ashley go down for their afternoon nap between three and three-thirty. We could actually have a conversation then."

That seems kind of late for a nap, but what do I know? I don't have kids. I'm also in no position to judge, given how late I got up today.

"Three-thirty? I'll see what I can do."

"Great. I'll see if I can have something ready for us to snack on while we chat."

The dogs and kids race back around behind her, this time one of the kids is riding the large pet.

"It seems like your hands are full. I'll bring something."

Darby gives me a tired smile. "That sounds great. Thank you."

"See you in a while."

Troy comes down the stairs in slacks, a pressed maroon shirt, and perfectly gelled hair—a stark contrast to the chaos down here. He stops mid-step when he sees me, doesn't say anything, but gives a slight nod before disappearing down the same hall his daughters and dog went a moment ago.

Darby starts to close the door

"Anything in particular you want me to pick up?" I ask her.

She turns back and tells her girls to stop running in the house before glancing back at me. "Surprise me. The more sugar, the better, though."

"Noted." I smile. "That definitely sounds good. See you in a bit."

We wave goodbye. As she closes the door, I head for the road and make it home just as fat, cold raindrops start to fall.

Before I get inside, a familiar car pulls up to my house.

Mia.

What does she want?

Looks like I'm about to find out.

26

Fleur

Thursday, early afternoon

Mia parks and races over to me. "Have I given you enough time to forgive me?"

"For lying to me over the course of *years*?"

She frowns, raindrops splattering all over her face.

"No." I march toward my house.

"Will you at least hear me out?" She chases after me.

"I did that the other day." I dig out my keys.

Just as I make to my porch, everything lights up bright white. Two seconds later, loud thunder rumbles. It's so strong, I can feel it.

Mia wraps her arms around herself. "That was close."

"Two miles." I unlock the door, let Zorro in, then step inside. "You really should get back in your car. The next strike could be closer."

Her expression falls. "Can't I come in here?"

"I'd rather you didn't."

"We need to talk."

"I don't see it that way."

"Please, Fleur." She begs with her eyes. "We've been friends forever."

"How much of that has been a lie?"

"None of it."

I cross my arms. "The fact that you can say that with a straight face deeply concerns me."

"It wasn't! I just didn't mention my friendship with Caroline—that doesn't change anything about *our* friendship. It's lasted the test of time *and* distance."

"Except you didn't bother to tell me that you made another best friend. You replaced me and didn't think it was worth mentioning." I reach for the door.

"Caroline didn't replace you."

"You didn't even mention you were going through the loss of a friend. That's the kind of thing you'd tell a bestie. Clearly, I don't make the cut. I'll let you know if I figure out anything new in her case. Or you can just listen to my podcast."

"Are you telling me you didn't make any friends in New York you didn't tell me about?"

"Yes."

"None? Really?"

"That's right. I had Ian, and he wanted to be my everything even though I was clearly just one of his many girlfriends. Any friends I had that I didn't mention to you were casual at best."

Mia frowns. "I really am sorry. Can we start over?"

"Not really."

"At the very least, I can help you with the mystery. Who better to fill in gaps than Caroline's best friend?"

"I'm already planning on talking with Darby today."

The sky lights up a blinding white, then thunder rumbles almost right away. It makes the walls shake. Heavy rainfall pelts the ground.

"Please let me in," Mia pleads.

I sigh in defeat. "Fine, come in."

She hurries inside, and I close the door just as the sky lights up again.

Mia peels off her coat and hangs it by the door. "Why are you talking to Darby?"

"Because she might be able to tell me something about Caroline that could point me in a helpful direction."

"Like I told you, she and Caroline grew apart as soon as Darby got pregnant with her oldest. With Shane's disinterest in kids, Caroline just couldn't handle spending time with Darby. That's when she and I started hanging out more. Because of my flexible schedule and Shane's long work hours, we had plenty of opportunities. The friendship just naturally happened."

I fill the tea kettle and put it on the stove. "Okay, so tell me what you know. Did Shane seem dedicated to her?"

"His first love was work."

"What makes you say that?"

"That's where he always was. Barely came home to sleep, much less spend any time with her. They were only together when they would go to church, and that was so he could look like a loving husband."

"You say he didn't want to have kids?"

"Right. It crushed Caroline, who wanted a baby more than anything."

"He never agreed to trying?"

"Yes, but he always put her off." Mia sits at the table and studies me. "Why all the questions about this?"

"I'm trying to get into both of their head spaces. Onto a different topic—have you gone into the murder room?"

"Thank God, no. I was worried I'd have to as an agent, but that was never an issue."

"What were Shane and Caroline like together?"

Mia shrugs. "Typical married couple."

"What does that mean? Were they all over each other or bickering all the time? Either could be considered normal, depending on the stereotype you're going after."

She sighs. "Closer to bickering, but it wasn't really like that entirely. It was like Caroline didn't want to cross him. She seemed eager to please, though when he wasn't around she complained about him a lot."

"Because he worked all the time?"

"That and the baby thing. She despised him for keeping her away from motherhood."

"Did they fight about that a lot?"

"I'm not sure." Mia looks deep in thought for a moment. "I mean, it isn't like I had many opportunities to see them together. But I do know she really resented him for it. I can't imagine they were too happy together with her feeling like that."

The teapot whistles, and I take it off the burner. "What about him? Did he resent her for pushing the issue?"

"She said he was annoyed anytime she brought it up. He accused her of being pushing, ungrateful, and whatnot."

"Ungrateful?" I pour steaming water into two mugs with tea bags, then hand her one before sitting across from her.

"He paid for the house and everything else, and he thought that should be enough. That him bringing home a paycheck was his job, and her job was to shut up and be happy about it."

"That's harsh. Did you hear him say that?"

Mia shakes her head. "That's what she told me."

"And they never came to an agreement about having kids?"

"Why do you keep asking?"

"Just trying to make sense of everything."

She sips from her mug. "Have you found anything interesting in here?"

"Just the tea."

"Not the kitchen. I mean in the house. Anything?"

"I think the cops took any evidence. If I'm going to find out what they have, I need to talk with them soon."

"If they'll tell you anything."

"The only way to know is to try."

"Keep in mind many of them are part of the cult."

"You aren't a fan of the Beacon of Truth Fellowship, I take it." I sip my drink.

Mia scowls. "Not even close. They're all crazy—they supported Shane making all of the decisions. Caroline wasn't given basic human agency in the marriage because of them. It wasn't a partnership, but a dictatorship."

That could be seen as motive if Caroline got pregnant against his wishes. Would the cops have covered that up for him? I need to find out what happened because Caroline was clearly looking forward to having a baby. A nursery that well stocked looked like a baby was already living there.

Then a thought strikes me. "Did they ever talk about fostering?"

Mia lifts a brow. "No. She wanted kids of her own, and he didn't want to foster. It was a sore subject for him."

"Even though they were both products of the foster care system? They might want to give back."

"No, they both had too many bad experiences in there."

I'm partially tempted to tell Mia about the nursery to see her reaction, but I want to keep this quiet for now. Once Mia finds out about it, she could tell others. For now, I want to see what people will tell me without knowing about the nursery.

The murder room.

Mia and I talk for a little while longer, but nothing she says gives me any hint as to what actually happened. It sounds like she thoroughly believes Shane is guilty, and that clearly colors everything she tells me.

She wants him to go down for this, so she's biased. That makes me wonder if I can believe anything she says about him.

I already know I can't trust her.

One thing I'm sure of, though, is she has no clue about the nursery. She kept a secret from me, and Caroline kept one from her. Interesting how that works.

What else are people hiding from each other?

I intend to get to the bottom of this. It's the only way to discover the truth.

It's a good thing I have a date with Darby soon. I tell Mia that I need to get going, and she grabs her coat without complaint. Apparently she thinks she won me over.

That's yet to be seen. I'm not sure I can trust *anyone*, least of all her. Not that I'm going to write off our longstanding friendship, but I'm not sure how well I actually know her anymore.

That's the problem with having had so much space between us for so long. It's like we have to start over, even though we never stopped communicating. My best bet might be to stop thinking of her as the Mia I knew, but rather as a new person.

It isn't like *I'm* the same person I was twelve years ago, and I can't expect her to be either. It's a lot to consider.

But for now I have just enough time to grab some food to bring to the meeting with my neighbor.

Mia pauses before stepping outside. "If you really want to get to the bottom of things, I think you should try to infiltrate the cult."

I jolt. "What makes you say that?"

She holds my gaze. "It's the only way any of them will open up to you. They don't talk to strangers."

That's definitely more than I planned when I decided to try and solve a murder.

Fake join a cult? That sounds dangerous.

I'll bring some wine and hope that loosens her up enough to spill more details than she might otherwise.

If that doesn't work, I might actually have to consider Mia's crazy idea.

27

Caroline

Before

It's ten minutes to checkout time. After that, I don't know where I'll go. Home doesn't feel safe. Not after last night, and not even considering Shane is most likely at work.

Unless he decided to stay home and wait for me.

My heart sinks at the thought. Maybe I should just walk away from everything. It isn't like I'd get anything if we divorced—he's a lawyer. Plus, he has the church on his side. They're more powerful than any judge around here.

I'm better off starting over. He doesn't want this baby, and he wouldn't even if it was his. He thinks it is, but as soon as the baby is born, he'll know better.

The problem is, I don't have anywhere to go. My only family is Shane and the members of the Beacon of Truth Fellowship.

I have nobody. Nowhere to go. Everything I know is at home, miserable as I am there.

The clock turns over, and now it's checkout time. I have to leave.

Without a plan.

If only my baby and I could move in with his or her dad. But that won't work. Not when he lives in our neighborhood.

Everyone will see me going into his house. They'll know.

Shane and the Beacon of Truth Fellowship will come after me.

That's why we have to meet at a hotel. It's too big of a risk.

Knock, knock!

"Housecleaning," someone calls from the other side of the door.

They're serious about their checkout time.

I grab my purse—the only thing I have with me—and open the door.

A shorter woman gives me a friendly smile. "Time to go. Have to clean now."

"Yeah, thanks." My voice cracks.

She gives me a sympathetic glance before stepping inside with her cart.

If I leave Shane, that's the kind of job I'll end up with. My adoptive parents didn't want me going to college, and I haven't worked since getting married. I have no education and no experience other than cleaning the house. I'm basically Shane's free maid.

I trudge down to the parking lot and round the corner where my car is hidden behind two dumpsters. At least it kept Shane from finding me last night. I had a few hours of rest and safety.

Now I have to face the music. Or at least get home and wait in anticipation all day.

That's going to be worse than seeing him when I get there.

Tears well in my eyes as I start the car and let it warm up.

The last thing I want to do is go home, but what other choice do I have?

If Shane isn't there, then someone from church likely will be. There's no way he didn't tell anyone about my disobedience. Especially not Alpha and Omega, the unforgiving leaders.

I hate my life. If it weren't for the precious life growing inside of me, I'd be tempted to end it all. But I finally have a baby to look forward to. Despite all the bad in my life, I've been given a blessing. I have to hold onto the hope that things will work out. Why else would I have been gifted this new life?

I draw a deep breath and pull out of the parking spot. Drive around the building at about five miles per hour. Wait extra-long before pulling onto the street.

Traffic is moving extra slow this morning. That's both good and bad. It's putting off the inevitable, but it also gives me more time to worry.

Whatever happens, I need to protect the baby. Shane won't.

He hasn't said anything, but he's not happy about the situation after having made it abundantly clear how he feels about having children.

Somehow I'm a defiant wife, even though the Beacon of Truth Fellowship wants all members to produce as many children as possible. The more babies, the more members. It's weird, but it makes sense to them.

I definitely want children. I've never been as excited about anything as I have about this baby growing inside of me. Obviously, I have my concerns and have to figure a few things out.

Shane is mad about this and has been even more temperamental than usual since finding out. The worst part is, he won't let me tell anyone. He doesn't want anyone else knowing until I'm showing, and unless the baby has a massive growth spurt, that won't be for a while.

Then there's the fact that he's going to flip when he realizes he isn't the father. If I'd have fallen for someone who looks more like my husband, that would've made that aspect of this easier. But I didn't, and it might be for the best. It gives me a strong reason to get out of my marriage, scary as the thought is.

I have no idea how I'll make it on my own, or if my baby's father will be able to help me out. But that's a problem to solve another day. When I get home, I'm going to have to figure out what I need to do next. The other day, I heard a statistic that shocked me—it takes a woman an average of eight attempts to leave a toxic relationship.

I don't have that kind of time—not before my little one gets here. I'm going to have to come up with a solid plan and stick with it. Even if it ends up only being a backup plan. I have to assume I'll be on my own. If I'm not ready for the worst case scenario, I'm not truly prepared.

By the time I turn into my neighborhood, I'm feeling a lot better about everything. I don't have any idea what I'm going to decide on, but at least I know I'm going to make up my mind about something. That's all that matters.

My heart stops when my house comes into sight.

Shane's car is out front. He's home.

That man never misses work. What's wrong?

This is a repeat of last night. Except I'm going to make sure this goes down differently.

Maybe what I need to do is whip back around and go to the library to figure out my next steps. There's no maybe about it—it's my only option.

I hit the brakes before I reach the driveway. I'm far enough away he can't see me even if he's looking out a window.

Heart hammering, I put my car into reverse and look back.

Slam on my brakes.

Someone is back there. Not just anyone.

Omega. The church leader is blocking me from turning around, standing with her arms spread out, taking up room on both sides of the street.

It takes my mind a moment to process it. By the time I do, Alpha is standing in front of my car. He and his wife are determined to stop me.

They have me trapped.

I can't go anywhere.

Not without running one of them down.

That's it. They'll have to move—neither one of them is a match for a motor vehicle. I may not stand a chance against them outside of my car, but inside is different story. I might get kicked out of the church, but at this point that would be a welcome change.

One less thing to disentangle myself from, especially given how hard they make it for anyone to leave without violating the agreement.

I glance back at Omega and forward at Alpha. Which one should I aim for? I would lose all my friends either way. Darby will be angry with me, but it isn't like we spend much time together anymore. Not since she had Ashley. We see even less of each other since she got pregnant again.

If I could tell her about my pregnancy, would we start to be friends again? I can't think like that. I'm escaping not only my marriage, but the Beacon of Truth Fellowship—and that includes everyone in it.

I'm making the choice to walk away from everyone I know, love, and hold dear.

This moment is one of no return. I can't go back from this.

But Alpha and Omega are making the decision easy on me, blocking me in like this.

I don't care who I go after. I press the gas, not even sure what gear my car is in.

The sedan bolts backward.

Omega it is.

I put more pressure on the pedal.

She stares with wide eyes as I quickly come near her. She glares at me and waves her hands around like a madwoman.

She'll soon be an injured madwoman if she doesn't get out of the way.

My leg jitters, wanting to stop. The last thing I want is to hurt anyone—even these oppressive church members who think I must obey them all, especially the men.

They'll both get a rude awakening in a moment.

Omega leaps out of the way just before I make contact.

Relief washes through me.

Not that I'm free yet.

Pounding sounds on the window next to me.

I glance over.

Alpha is hitting the window and ordering me to pull over.

Not a chance.

On the other side, Omega punches the window. Hard. It cracks like a little spider web. Then again. She may be stronger than her husband.

They're going to break in and drag me away.

I scream for them to stop.

Then I switch the car into Drive and hit the gas. My head hits the headrest, but I don't slow down.

Thunk!

A round dent now decorates my back window.

Thunk!

A rock hits the glass mere inches from the dent.

They're throwing rocks at my car!

These people have lost their minds.

Thunk!

That one hits one of the other dents and shatters the window. Glass shards trickle down.

Another hits the trunk.

They aren't going to stop. I don't know how they're keeping up.

I need to get out of the neighborhood where I can drive faster. There's too big a chance of a child or pet running into the road if I speed away.

Thunk! Crash!

That rock shatters my back window and hits the back of my seat.

Troy leaps out in front of me.

These nut jobs are everywhere!

I slam on the brakes.

They've left me with only one option. I fling open the door and get out of the car.

Then I run.

28

Fleur

Thursday, late afternoon

The wine bottle sticks out of my purse as I walk up Darby's driveway. I've found nothing gets people talking quite like a glass of wine. I know these people are religious, so hopefully she isn't opposed to drinking it. However, should she be, I hope the super sugary donuts in my hand—not from Sally's bakery—will do the trick. Sugar isn't alcohol, but it does seem to come in as a nice second when someone doesn't want the first.

I balance the box of sweets in one hand as I ring the doorbell with the other.

No clatter of footsteps sound this time. That's right, the kids are napping. Maybe I should have knocked. If the chime wakes them, I'll lose my chance to talk with Darby alone.

I'm about to knock when she opens the door.

"Sorry about the doorbell. I hope it didn't wake Ashley and Emma."

"No worries." She gives me a tired smile. "The sound goes to the phones, not through the house."

"Smart." I hold out the pink box. "I hope you like donuts."

Her smile widens. "That sounds so good! Thank you."

"It's the least I can do after all you've done for me. Now I have a bed I can sleep in. It's heavenly compared to the couch."

"Nice. You'll have to remind me to show you how the other bed looks in our guest room."

"I wouldn't miss it." I close the door behind me.

Darby leads me through a well decorated living room into a sparkly kitchen full of the latest gadgets. She nods toward the table. "You can put the box there. I'll get some plates. Do you drink milk? I also have oat milk because so many people have allergies."

"I brought something better." I nudge my purse so the top of the wine bottle is more obvious.

Her eyes widen. "Oh, wow. I think I'll get milk out anyway."

My heart sinks a little. It sounds like she doesn't go near adult drinks. At least she looks excited about the donuts. I'm glad I went out of town and found the big chain with the fancy options. The workers were friendly, unlike some places around here.

Darby sets small plates and glasses of milk on the table before opening the box. "These look amazing!"

"Take whatever you want. You can also set some aside for your kids if you'd like."

Her gaze darts around. "Okay."

"Does Troy not like them having sugar?"

She chews on her lower lip. "Not often, but every once in a while is fine. It's been a few days, so I'm sure he won't say anything."

"Even so, you're their mom. You have an equal say."

She swallows. "This one is amazing! You should have the other. I think my taste buds might melt off."

Clearly she doesn't want to talk about the fact that she doesn't have a say in her household regarding her own children. I can't imagine living like that. Sure, Ian wasn't perfect—not by a long shot—and he demanded his way at times, but it wasn't like he ran the show. We were partners in our relationship.

It just turned out that I wasn't the only one he had a relationship with, and he also had no intention of having a family or getting married.

Good riddance. But I'd never have stayed as long as I did if he was a pushy tyrant.

Or would I have? I can't honestly say what I would or wouldn't do in someone else's shoes. I have no idea what Darby's life has been like, especially if she grew up in a cult.

I shudder at the thought.

"Are you okay?" Darby asks, her eyes full of concern.

"Yeah, great." I pull myself to the present. I'm here to talk about Caroline's murder. "So, how well did you know Caroline?"

Darby coughs, drinks some milk.

"Sorry. Should I have not asked about her?"

"It's fine." Darby wipes her mouth. "Just went down the wrong pipe."

"You two were best friends?"

"Right. We go way back."

Troy appears around the corner. He leans against the wall, doesn't say anything.

I turn to him. "Do you want a donut?"

He shakes his head.

Darby dabs her mouth with a napkin again. "He likes to watch his sugar intake."

"Keto diet?" I ask.

"No." He shoots his wife a glare. "Just treating my body like a temple."

Pink colors her cheeks.

"A treat here and there is good for the soul." I reach for a bacon-covered maple bar.

Troy's brows draw together.

I turn my attention back to Darby. "How far back did you and Caroline go?"

Darby's eyes dart toward her husband again. "We knew each other in school. How are you settling into the house?"

"It's great. Did you two grow up around here?"

"We did." She eyes the donut box but doesn't reach for any.

"What year were you?"

Darby plays with her napkin, twisting it. "We were a year ahead of your sister. That was such a tragedy."

It takes me a moment to recover. I wasn't expecting the conversation to go in that direction. "You knew Lourdes?"

"Didn't everyone?"

"I suppose."

"It's hard to believe she's never been found."

A lump forms in my throat, as it often does when someone unexpectedly brings up my sister in conversation. "I think her case will be solved one day."

"I sure hope so."

I turn to Troy, who hasn't budged from his spot. "Did you know her?"

"Knew of her."

"Were you in the same grade as Darby and Caroline?"

He shakes his head.

Darby picks up her glass. "Troy was two years ahead of us."

"Is that how you two met?"

"We met through church," Darby says. "My parents introduced us."

"How romantic." I don't even try to keep the sarcasm from my tone.

Neither responds.

This conversation is going to go nowhere as long as Troy continues hovering.

I stare at him, hoping he'll take the hint.

He doesn't.

"Anyone want some wine?" I pull out the bottle and wait for his response.

Darby rises. "I'm going to have some ice water. Do you want some?"

"No," I say to her, but keep my gaze on him.

He steps away from the wall. "I'll have some wine."

So much for being concerned about his sugar intake. Now I'm curious why Darby won't have any since her aversion clearly isn't religious.

"Great." I leap up. "Where do you keep the corkscrew?"

"I'll get it." He takes the bottle to the counter and turns his back to us.

I try to see what he's doing, but he's blocking my view of the wine bottle.

Darby sits with her ice water.

"Are you sure you don't want any?" I ask.

"I am."

These people are impossible to figure out, and I've dealt with some tough nuts to crack in my time interviewing people for the podcast.

"Do you prefer white wine?" I ask.

She places a hand on her stomach. "I'm expecting again. We've been blessed with a third."

"Hopefully this time a boy." Troy shoots her an annoyed glance.

"Isn't Emma only one?" I ask.

"We like to keep them close." Troy hands me a glass and sits with one of his own.

I stare at my glass, not trusting he hasn't done something to it. Given the way he's insisting on being in the middle of this conversation, I'm not about to trust the man. "Do you work at home?"

He takes a big swig of his drink. "I work remotely when I can."

"That must be nice being able to spend so much time with your family."

His only response is to grunt.

Darby twirls her glass of ice water, now sitting with a perfectly straight back. Her gaze goes back and forth between her husband and me.

Troy taps his finger on the table. Repeatedly.

This is going nowhere fast, and I still want to talk with the police to see if I can get anything out of them. Even if some of them are part of the cult, they can't all be.

I push my chair back and rise. "I'm so glad we could spend some time getting to know each other, but I should get going. Feel free to keep the donuts and share them with your girls."

Troy scowls but doesn't say anything.

Darby glances back and forth between us before landing her gaze on me. "Let me show you to the door."

I thank her, and when we reach the door she whispers an apology to me.

"Don't worry about it. We'll talk later. Maybe at my house?"

She nods furiously.

"Great. Text me a time that works for you. You can bring the girls, and they can play with Zorro in the backyard while we talk."

Darby gives me a wide smile and closes the door behind me.

I hope I can get more from the police.

29

Fleur

Thursday, early evening

I've been sitting in the waiting room at the police department for at least an hour. It feels like much longer, especially with the grungy guy, who smells like a swamp, across from me. He keeps leering and doesn't even back down when I stare at him.

He gets called back before me, even though I've been waiting longer. Maybe the cop he needs to talk to is less busy than the one I'm waiting on?

More likely, the detectives are hoping I'll go away. Considering how little attention Caroline's murder has gotten and the fact that a good portion of the officers are part of the cult, that wouldn't surprise me.

I'll just keep waiting, even if I need to wait for a shift change. Perhaps I'll get a different cop—one who will be more willing to speak openly with me.

A little later, swamp guy returns to the waiting room and leaves. Not without staring at me, of course.

Annoyed, I return to the receptionist.

He glances up at me. "Can I help you?"

"I'm still waiting to speak with someone about the Caroline Porter case."

"Yes, you're on the waiting list."

"That guy who just left got here after me."

"Right."

"So, why am I still waiting?"

He gestures toward the sitting area. "You aren't the only one."

"They've *all* been here less time than me."

"I'm sure you'll be called next."

An officer opens the door.

I give her a pleading look.

She calls someone else.

I glare at the receptionist. "Are you still going to deny I'm being put off?"

He taps keys on his keyboard, but I'm sure it has nothing to do with me or how long I've been waiting. "It isn't up to me."

"Surely there must be someone you can talk to."

"It won't help."

"Maybe it would."

"Please take a seat." He points toward the uncomfortable chairs.

"I think I'll wait here."

"This area is for new arrivals."

I make a point of glancing around. "There aren't any."

"Have a seat."

"No, thank you."

His eyebrows draw together.

I don't budge.

"Fine," he says. "Wait here. But when someone walks through the door, you'll need to move."

"Sure." I turn my back to him and lean against the counter.

He sighs loudly, but I pretend not to hear him.

Another person gets called back. This is getting ridiculous.

Just as the door is about to close, I stick my foot over and block it. Then I turn slightly to see if the receptionist notices.

He doesn't. Neither does anyone in the waiting room.

Blood rushes in my ears. I inch the door a little more.

Nobody so much as glances over.

I inch it again. Wait.

After looking all around, I grab the door, step inside, then let it close behind me.

I'm in.

The receptionist is looking at something on his phone—wholly inappropriate for someone on the clock, paid with tax dollars—and the subject matter is even more unsuitable for public viewing. But that means he isn't paying attention to me.

Perfect.

I creep down the hall. Voices sound from several directions behind ajar doors in various places. I glance around, not sure what I'm looking for. This isn't a large town, so it's possible they have filing systems in actual filing cabinets unlike larger cities which would have moved it all online long ago.

There's only one way to find out.

I make my way to the end of the hall that has the least chatter—less chance of running into someone.

Behind one door, I hear someone say Caroline Porter.

My breath hitches, and I press myself against the wall and cup my ear, leaning toward the slightly open door.

"We have to tell that podcaster something," says a man with a deep voice.

"She'll eventually leave if we don't go get her." This man's voice is a few octaves higher.

"Have you checked out her podcast? That witch get things done. She's helped solve numerous cold cases."

Witch? I could probably be called worse.

"Doesn't mean she'll get the best of us."

"It also doesn't mean she won't. She's so determined to bring justice to the skank that she moved into their house! Who does that?"

A sigh sounds from the room.

"What do you propose we do? I've never dealt with anything like this."

"We continue to keep things under wraps, that's what."

"How? That podcaster is already poking around. We have to tell her something."

"Troy already made sure his wife won't say anything. We're good on that front."

"But what are *we* going to tell her?"

"To mind her own bloody business."

A snort. "You really think that'll work? This podcaster isn't a righteous woman. She won't obey us just because we're men."

"But we're police. She has to honor that."

"She'll dig deeper if she doesn't believe us. We're dealing with a Jezebel spirit."

"What's she gonna find? It isn't like she can get in here."

They both laugh.

So do I, but silently.

"Seriously, though. We need to do something. The chief won't be happy about us leaving someone sitting out there this long."

"Fair point. We'll talk to her but won't give her any information. Our prerogative will be to see what she knows. We need to figure out that much, anyway."

"Anything else?"

"We'll focus on that for now. After our shift, we'll have to speak with Alpha and Omega to plan our next steps."

"Good thinking."

Alpha and Omega? Is that what they call their god? Or is that the name of a cult leader? If they're looking for answers, it has to be a person. Unless they're referring to prayer.

Either way, they have no intention of telling me anything useful, and they only want to squeeze me for information.

That's so backward. It also screams of a coverup.

Footsteps sound behind me.

I whip around.

The receptionist. He puts his hands on his hips. "What are you doing here?"

"Looking for the bathroom. I guess it isn't this way?"

"How did you get in here?" His nostrils flare.

"You'd know if you hadn't been so busy on your phone." I cock a brow.

His face flushes crimson. "You need to leave."

"Right. You don't mention seeing me here, and I won't say anything about what was on your screen during your work shift."

Somehow his face turns an even deeper shade of red. "Fine. Go."

"Gladly. I got what I needed, anyway." I push past him then head back the way I came.

He follows me all the way to the front door, which he holds open for me.

"What a gentleman."

"Goodbye, Ms. Bardot."

I wave, my mind racing with the new information.

One thing is certain—Mia was right about me needing to break into the cult. I'm going to have to be careful, or they'll see right through me.

But it's the only way I'll get answers.

30

The Watcher

Speaking with Alpha and Omega

The dim room has never seemed more ominous. Even the hundred or so flickering candles do nothing to change the ambiance. Normally I find this room calming, but now it's anything but relaxing.

Creak.

My heart leaps into my throat. Has that door always been so noisy? Or am I jumpy? Maybe a bit of both.

Alpha steps into the doorway, his long, flowy gown seeming darker than usual. He turns slowly to me. "Come in, my child."

"Yes, your grace." I barely manage to keep my voice steady. If he can see my nervousness, he doesn't indicate it.

Inside the retreat room, Alpha's wife Omega sits on a mat. It's brighter in here, though not by much. The walls are painted a pale purple—Omega's choice—and the glow of the candles is softer in here. The glittery ceiling offers a little cheer.

Alpha gestures toward another mat.

I sit quickly and cross my legs, though it's harder as I get older. Not that I'm old. Not even close, but no matter how much I focus on spiritual things, my body is still tethered to the earth and its various laws. Age is kind to nobody other than children.

Silence settles around us. As tempting as it is to speak first, I know I must wait.

No one can speak before Alpha or Omega, and they're both here.

Despite the obvious attempts at a light atmosphere, it's tense. Really tense.

I joined this group because they showed it to me in the light of being able to be the king of my castle. If I joined, I would rule my tiny kingdom at home. They would provide me with a wife who would happily obey all of my wishes.

Who wouldn't want that? It's a dream come true.

There's one major problem. I have to let these people choose my mate for me. Not only that, but outside of our home, I am not the ruler. These two people holding a staring contest with me are my superiors.

Not a word of this was mentioned before I joined. Funny how that works. They wait to talk about obedience until after they have you. Then there's a matter of that membership agreement. It's literally going to cost my soul to get out of that thing.

Now there's another issue I have with this group, and that's likely why I'm here. Word has probably gotten out that the woman I'm in love with and want as my slave—I mean wife—is not a member of our community.

Yet.

That's a massive distinction. All I need is to get her on the inside, convince her to join.

Then I'll be golden. We all will.

Well, mostly. There are a few other hitches to that plan, but I can deal with those later. Right now, I have enough on my plate.

Omega clears her throat. "I imagine you're wondering why we called you in today."

So dramatic.

I bite back a sarcastic reply, only blinking for a few moments. Two can play at this staring, waiting game. "I have my suspicions."

"Do you?" Alpha straightens his back.

"You know me. Always thinking."

They both nod.

A few of the flames flicker, causing an ominous shadow behind my two leaders.

It's pretty spooky, but I don't so much as flinch.

Neither do they.

Omega leans forward, her long hair getting in her face. "Why do you think we brought you here?"

This is a dangerous question. If I answer wrong, and it turns out they aren't aware of my affections, I could have serious consequences.

Sometimes I hate this life.

"My wife asked you a question," Alpha says.

"I'd rather hear from you two. What importance do my words hold?"

They exchange a meaningful glance.

Apparently my words were the right choice.

Omega turns to me. "We know of your intentions."

Why wouldn't they?

I nod, waiting for her to go on. I'm still not sure they're referring to what my actual intentions are. That's yet to be seen.

Alpha adjusts his seating position. "You think you can convince her to join us?"

They *do* know my intentions.

"Yes. I'm already working on it."

"And?"

"These things take time."

"Clearly."

They both stare at me expectantly.

"What of the other issue?" Alpha raises both eyebrows.

"It's under control."

"Meaning?"

"Meaning I can handle it."

"Details." Omega gives me a death stare that sends a shiver down my spine. Of the two, she's easily the scarier one.

"I'd rather wait until we're a little further along in the process."

She taps a nail on her mat. "That isn't good enough."

"It's going to have to be for now."

Alpha and Omega exchange another look, this one indecipherable. She turns back to me. "You have one week."

"One week? To pull all of this together?"

The woman blinks slowly. "To return and give us all the details we need. You have seven days to do what you feel must be kept in confidence, and then you tell us everything. Not one thing gets left out. The more you've accomplished, the better for your case."

"Yes, your grace." My chest tightens. A week isn't long enough.

Except it's going to have to be. I don't have any other choice.

It's time to up my game.

Significantly.

31

Fleur

Friday afternoon

D*ing!*
 I turn my attention toward the restaurant door. A couple holding hands walks inside.

Not Emmett. I'm meeting him for lunch to see what I can find out from him about Caroline and Shane. Meeting for lunch seemed less romantic—I don't want to send the wrong signals. If I took him up on his suggestion for dinner, that would have. Luckily he was available for lunch, though I've been waiting ten minutes and he still isn't here.

I'm doing everything I can to avoid giving off date vibes—my hair is slightly messy, my clothes aren't particularly great although I'm professional. This is an interview, after all.

A worker appears and calls my name. I rise and glance around. Looks like I'm going to need to text Emmett and let him know I'm already at the table.

Ding!

He rushes over, giving me that gorgeous smile of his. "Sorry I'm late!"

"No problem." I hate how attracted to him I am. It almost makes me rethink my stance on not getting involved with people in cases I'm investigating.

But no. I won't budge. It could compromise my career someday, and that's not a risk I'm willing to take. Everything I do with my podcast and books has to be above board.

The worker shows us halfway through the restaurant before taking us to a table with a view of the lake it sits next to.

So much for not being romantic. At least there aren't candles and dim lights. The bright afternoon sun lights up the table as though summer was still hanging on instead of pushing toward Halloween.

"My audition ran late," Emmett says, after we have the menus.

"Hopefully that's promising." I glance over the lunch selections.

He shrugs. "You never know."

"What role is this one for?"

"Some kind of commercial again. They didn't give a lot of details."

"Is that typical?"

"Sometimes. If it's a new product, the companies can be pretty hush-hush about everything. Just depends."

"How do you feel you did?" The reason I keep asking questions is because I've found it warms people up to talk about themselves before answering questions for me. And in this case, Emmett doesn't know that's why we're here.

He talks about the performance he gave, and I nod along like I know anything about what he's saying. His world is so different from mine, even though technically we're both in entertainment. I'm behind a screen most of the time and rarely have to worry about how I look. Even when my podcast is on video, I'm not on screen. I have my logo up with the sound playing. People listen to me, they don't watch—unless I'm being interviewed, which does happen from time to time.

We talk about Emmett's career until the food arrives.

Once we're a few bites in, I get to the point. "Do you have any theories about Caroline's death?"

He chokes but recovers quickly.

"Sorry. I didn't mean to make you choke."

Emmett wipes his mouth with a napkin. "No, it's fine. Just went down the wrong way."

"You don't mind talking about her?"

"Not at all."

"So, *do* you have any theories?"

He takes a sip of his wine. "Who doesn't?"

"Seems like a lot of people. I can hardly find anything online about any of this."

"Is that odd?"

"For almost nothing to be written about the murder of a pretty, young mom-to-be? Definitely."

He doesn't so much as flinch at the mention of her pregnancy. Either he already knew, or he doesn't find it surprising.

I want to yell for him to answer, but instead I just give him a bland smile.

Emmett takes another sip of his drink. "I'm not really active in the true crime community, so I wouldn't know."

"This is the kind of crime people get worked up about. You can easily find a number of documentaries on similar cases if you have any streaming service."

He nods, looking thoughtful.

"You don't have any idea why nobody's talking about Caroline?"

"She and Shane were fairly private people."

"But he's missing, too," I point out. "It isn't like he's around to orchestrate any of this staying out of the press. Seems like someone else would be pulling strings like that. Don't you think?"

He clears his throat. "Well, they do belong to a church. Maybe they have something to do with that. I wonder if they could help?"

I shake my head, thinking back to the conversation between the cops I overheard yesterday.

"You don't think so?"

"If they want to keep things quiet, that must mean they have something to hide."

"Only from outsiders."

I study him. "Are you saying you think I should try to get inside the group?"

"That's not what I said."

"It's what you insinuated."

"More like how you took it." His eyes sparkle, like he's enjoying the banter.

"How do you suppose I would go about something like that? Assuming I decide to go that route."

Emmett looks deep in thought. "I imagine you'd have to be interested in joining."

"Yeah, feigning interest would likely be best."

"I said *be* interested."

"Potato, pah-tah-to."

He shakes his head. "They'd see right through you if you weren't genuine."

"What makes you say that?"

"I've seen curious people try to get in. They're always denied access."

"Always? That seems like a bold statement."

"It's what I've seen, like I said."

"Do people try to get in often?"

He shrugs.

"A church that denies access?"

"They don't deny people with a genuine interest. Only people who aren't really believers."

"And what are you?"

"An actor." He flashes a disarming smile.

Feeling warm, I sip my water. "You never answered my question. Do you have a theory about Caroline's murder?"

"I don't know what happened."

"Obviously. That's the whole point of a theory."

He takes the last bite of his food. "A lot of people point fingers at Shane. Why else would he just disappear? He must have something to hide. Besides, don't they say it's always the husband?"

"Or boyfriend."

"She's married."

"Married people have boyfriends and girlfriends."

"Not in the Beacon of Truth Fellowship."

I balk. "That's where you're wrong."

Emmett lifts a brow.

"Statistically, there's no difference between religious and nonreligious couples as far as infidelity and divorce."

He straightens his back. "Statistics show that married religious people have better sex lives."

"Those stats are being overturned as better studies come out."

"Really?" He leans forward. "Tell me more."

I feel like the tables have turned and I'm now being interviewed, but I don't really care. I'm happy to share new stats to prove him wrong. "Newer studies prove married religious couples aren't actually having better experiences in the bedroom. They might be having more frequent encounters, and that's because of their cultural expectations, but they're of worse quality because the women's needs are largely being ignored—it's all about the male release in most religious settings."

"Male release?" He snorts.

"It's tacky wording for sure, but it's not mine. The language is directly from numerous religious marriage books aimed at women, who buy and read the majority of those books. Those pages are full of advice that has largely been proven harmful to marriages. Since the advice is so statistically bad, desperate wives run out to buy even more of those books in hopes of improving their marriages and quality of life. As with everything else, follow the money and you'll find your answers—doling out bad marriage advice fills the pockets of the unscrupulous publishers."

"Sounds like you've done your homework."

It's my turn to shrug. "I like to keep up on relevant studies that affect my cases. It just happens this is an area getting a lot of attention lately."

"Let me guess," he says. "There are podcasts on the subject."

"Of course. But let's get back to Caroline. You said you were friends?"

"Right."

"How close would you say you were?"

He shrugs.

I swear I'm going to scream if he does that one more time. "How about on a scale of one to ten? Ten being you were her best friend ever."

"Three? Four?"

"So, you guys talked but not too deeply?"

"I guess."

"What is it with you and one word answers?" I exclaim.

"That was two words. Can we talk about something else?"

"Great idea. What do you think happened to Shane?"

Emmett's shoulders slump. "That isn't really a change in subject."

"No? Were you friends with him?"

"Hardly."

"Then it's a different subject."

He glances at his watch. "You know what? I have to get going. We'll have to do this again sometime."

I've gotten nothing out of him. I need to get him talking before he leaves. "What should I do to make sure I get an in with the Beacon of Truth Fellowship?"

"What makes you think I know?"

"You've been living here longer and dealing with the group."

He waves the server over. "Doesn't mean I have an in."

"You must have an idea."

"Not really."

I'm going to have to figure out a different way to get the information I need or keep looking for someone who will actually open up. Clearly, Emmett isn't as helpful as I'd hoped.

"Wait," he says. "I have an idea."

I give him a suspicious glance. "What?"

"We could work together on trying to get inside the community."

"Are you serious?"

"Yes."

"What's in it for you?"

Surprisingly, he doesn't shrug. "It could be fun."

I don't bother to hide my dubious expression.

"No, really. It'd be like practicing for a role—but this one would have real world consequences."

"Meaning?"

He tilts his head. "Have you met these people? They have their hands in every corner of this town."

"See, that's so weird to me. I grew up here, and nothing like that existed. It almost makes me wonder how different everything would be if Lourdes had never disappeared."

"I have no doubt it would be very different."

"Excuse me?" I give him a double take and feel blood drain from my face.

"Oh, I don't mean anything sinister. Only that people needed hope afterward. Your sister changed this town, and the group was more than happy to step up and meet a need. It started with one person, then another, and sometime after you moved, they had changed everything even more than your sister. If she'd never disappeared, they never would have gotten a foothold in town."

I stare at him in disbelief.

Before I can find my voice, he gives the server a credit card and says he's paying for both of our meals.

32

Caroline

Before

It feels like I've been on the run for days, but it's barely nightfall. I've been jumping at every noise and movement, worried either Shane or one of the other guys from the Beacon of Truth Fellowship is going to grab me and force me back home.

I can't believe this is happening. I'll never be able to go back home. How can I? Even if Shane does go back to work—he has to at some point—he's sure to have someone staking out the house.

I'm going to have to start over with nothing. Unless I can find someone to start over with. I press my palm against my stomach.

"Do you think your daddy will let us in his place?"

That's my only option—asking him. Not that I can call him up. I had to leave everything in the car, including my purse which held my phone. I'm lucky to have my coat. If the afternoon had been much warmer, I might not have had that.

Now that I have the cover of darkness, I make my way back to the neighborhood. It's a well-lit community, making it harder to stay completely hidden. What once brought me comfort could now be my downfall. Between the porch lights and streetlights, I have to be extremely careful not to be seen.

I dart from tree to tree to bush, staying in the shadows as much as possible. Eventually, I make it to my house.

No. It's Shane's house. I can't call it home any longer. The church has always said it's his, despite my name also being on the mortgage. They say that because the husband is the leader of his own tiny kingdom, and everything in that kingdom belongs to him.

It's actually a relief that I won't have to raise my child in that oppressive culture. We both have value even though we aren't men, and we will live like it!

The thought actually sends a brief wave of warmth through me. This is a new beginning for both of us. We can live out the lives we were meant to live, without being controlled in any way, shape, or form.

Not that I can get excited yet. No, I need to get away. Then I'll probably have to watch my back for a while, at least until I put enough distance between me and them. My status as a runaway wife will give him the freedom to start over with a new wife, one who will make him happier.

As long as I can get free, I don't care.

I give the house one last glance before continuing down the street. My lover's house isn't far, but right now it feels like it may as well be miles in the desert.

The sound of car tires makes me jolt. I leap behind the nearest tree, making sure I can't be seen at all, not even my shadow.

Every muscle in my body seizes momentarily.

I know that car.

It pulls into the same driveway I've used every day for years.

My mouth dries, and my hands shake.

Things are really serious now.

I wait, unable to move as the expensive vehicle parks next to Shane's.

Omega steps out from the driver's side, and Alpha from the passenger side.

My stomach lurches even though I know I'm breaking free from this life and these people will have no more power over me. Seeing them is like when I was a kid and got sent to the principal's office—only this is much, much worse.

Now I have to be even more careful. If they get ahold of me...

I shudder at the thought. I can't even let my mind go there.

It won't happen. I'm going to find a way out of the reach of the Beacon of Truth Fellowship. Get far from where they hold so much power, where I can't go anywhere without running into someone from the large group.

They will all be on the lookout for me.

I wait for the leaders to go inside after Shane opens the door and welcomes them.

The door closes, giving more space between them and me.

Still I don't budge.

Terror grips me. If they see me, it's over. I'm done for.

I'm almost tempted to give myself over to them so I don't have to keep running. It would be easier that way.

No. I can't do that. I'm so close to escape. It's dark, cold, and most people are inside staying warm. Not many will be looking outside for someone running for her life.

Except my husband and Alpha and Omega could be.

My stomach lurches again. This time I'm not sure I can keep it under control. Somehow I manage to keep what small amount of food is in my stomach down.

I wait, watching the house for what feels like hours but is probably only a minute or two. Until I'm sure they aren't going to jump out and grab me.

Not that I think I'll ever be safe from that. Even if I move across the country, there's always the risk of one of them finding me.

Finally, I get my feet to move. I glance all around, not seeing anyone anywhere.

Thunder rumbles in the distance.

Good. That makes it even more likely people will stay inside.

It takes at least twice as long as it normally would to make the trek. I pass Darby's house, a wave of regret washing through me. If only I hadn't pulled away from her after she got pregnant the first time. I'd thought it was painful seeing my friend living the dream I wanted—not only expecting a baby, but also having a doting husband who actually *wanted* kids with her—but barely having her in my life hurt even more.

When I reach my destination, I stare at the house, unable to move. I've never actually been inside. We just talk like normal neighbors when people are around, and we meet up in other places like the hotel.

He isn't expecting me. What if he has company?

What if someone from the church is there?

My blood runs cold at the thought. But why would they? They don't know we have a relationship.

Or do they? What if one of the members works at the hotel, and I didn't realize it? It isn't like he would know either.

I take a deep breath. This is my only chance at freedom. Even if he doesn't want a relationship with me beyond what we've had, at least he could take me to a bus or train station to get out of town.

It's a risk I have to take.

My legs shake as I walk up to his house. I stop at the door and stare at it, my knees threatening to give out from under me.

I knock.

Nothing.

He has to be home.

I knock louder.

Footsteps sound on the other side.

This is it. My fate is about to be determined.

The deadbolt clicks. The knob turns.

Slowly the door opens.

Emmett appears in front of me. His eyes widen with surprise, then they fill with concern. "Are you okay, Caroline?"

I shake my head, tears blurring my vision.

He pulls me inside then locks the door behind us.

33

Fleur

Friday, late afternoon

I press publish on my latest podcast episode, not that I have much of an update. Mostly I talk about my experience going through the items in the house, and I make a few minor things sound more interesting than they are. It'll be enough to satisfy the curiosity of my listeners for now and also build interest for future episodes.

If I don't make any progress trying to get inside the cult—not something I can broadcast to the public, for obvious reasons—then I might have to bring to light the fact that Caroline and Shane were expecting a baby.

That *has* to drum up more interest in the case. The police might be more than happy to ignore that fact, but not my listeners. This will bring more attention to Caroline from the general public. Aside from a missing or murdered child, little else will stir up ire in people than a dead pregnant woman. For good reason.

It's sickening that murder is such a high cause of death for pregnant women.

I'm tempted to check my stats on the episode, but it's best I put it out of my mind for now. What I need to do is convince Darby that I want to join their cult.

I've only been back in town for less than a week, so they could be suspicious. It wouldn't surprise me if they were, but hopefully I've shown Darby I'm genuine. She must have some faith in me since I'm trying to solve her friend's murder. A murder which has been ignored for two years.

I send her a quick text to see if she's home.

She replies, saying that her girls should be sleeping for another hour.

Perfect. Maybe this is my lucky day.

I tell her I'll be right over, then I let Zorro out to relieve himself before heading to Darby's. With any luck, her husband won't be working remotely today. Regardless, I'm going to express interest in the Beacon of Truth Fellowship. What could go wrong?

Plenty, I'm sure. If things get weird again, I'll leave and find someone else to talk about joining the group. If they've infiltrated the town, it should be easy to find other members. I grew up here, so people should trust me. Although it's pretty obvious everyone thinks of me as an outsider now, especially with my sister missing and both my parents dead.

That doesn't even take into consideration the fact that I'm drawing worldwide attention to a case they seem to want hidden—or at least certain members of the group want to keep under wraps.

If I'm successful, my infiltration will be a balancing act. They might even try to stop me from posting episodes about Caroline. But I'll deal with that when I get to it, if it becomes an issue.

Darby opens her front door before I have a chance to knock.

She must be afraid I'll accidentally ring the doorbell again. Or maybe she doesn't want Troy knowing that I'm here.

I'm all for that option.

She gives me a wide smile as she ushers me in. "How are you, Fleur?"

"Not bad. You?"

"Tired, but that's what happens when I chase two small girls all morning." She closes and locks the door.

"While pregnant."

Her eyes widen for a moment. "Oh, right. I forgot you knew. Yes, that certainly adds to it. Are you hungry? We still have some of your donuts left. Troy doesn't want the girls eating them, but I've let them have a bite here and there."

"I'm glad they can enjoy them, but no, I don't need any food. I had a big lunch."

"Did you have a good conversation with Emmett?"

I hesitate. Did I mention that to her?

Darby smiles again. "I saw him outside earlier, and he mentioned it."

"Oh, gotcha. We had a good time. I'm enjoying getting to know the neighbors who are actually friendly."

"Right. Well, let's have a seat. Do you want some tea? Water?"

"No, honestly I'm fine."

I follow her to a family room. She picks up a few random toys and gestures for me to take a seat. I pick the loveseat. It'll force us to sit closer, and I won't have to talk loudly, ensuring her husband won't easily be able to eavesdrop.

Maybe I'm being overly cautious, but I don't think so. The more I learn about this group, the more secretive I realize they are. They clearly don't want me meddling.

Darby collapses next to me and sighs loudly. "How are you settling into the house? Is it feeling more like your own now?"

"I'm getting there. It does help having my own bed to sleep in."

"I can imagine. Have you gone into Caroline's craft room?"

My pulse races. Do I dare show my cards? It might be worth it to see her reaction. Not only that, but it'll show her that I'm opening up to her. I lean toward her. "It's not a craft room."

Her mouth gapes, and her pupils dilate. "It isn't?"

I shake my head, continuing to study her. The shock seems genuine. She can't fake her pupils.

Darby looks around and leans closer. "What is it?"

Once I tell her, I can't undo that. But at the same time, it isn't like the cops don't know.

"Well?" Her eyes are wide as saucers.

"It's a nursery."

She doesn't move, doesn't even blink for a moment. "As in a baby nursery?"

"Right. Fully stocked."

Darby leans back and brushes some hair from her face. "She was pregnant?"

"It appears that way. Either that, or she was into that manifesting stuff and trying to make it happen."

"Oh, there's no way she was into manifesting. That's of the devil."

"Is it?" I try to look deeply concerned, even though I have no opinions on manifesting either way, except that I'm pretty sure it isn't demonic. But I can't let her know that. If I want in, I have to at least pretend to drink the Kool-Aid.

"Without a doubt. We can't make our own destiny—how prideful do you think someone has to be to believe that? We as people lack understanding, and our hearts are deceitful more than anything else in the world. They can't be trusted."

"But if you follow God and scriptures, shouldn't you be able to trust your heart?"

Her eyes manage to grow even wider. "Never! We have to trust our superiors to tell us what to do."

"But aren't their hearts deceitful too? They're only people, after all."

"They have divine wisdom for people below them."

My mind spins, trying to keep up with the mental gymnastics. "Always?"

"Of course."

"But what about the highest person? Who do they turn to?"

"God."

"But his or her heart would also be deceived."

Darby shakes her head. "What's with all the questions?"

I take a deep breath and look around the room like I'm deep in thought. "I suppose it's due to being back in my hometown. It reminds me that not only is Lourdes still missing, but now my parents are dead too. It's hard not to think about the meaning of life."

She squeezes my hand. "That must be so hard. Do you have any family?"

"My Mimi Perle is about an hour away. I've been thinking I should swing by and see how she's doing. I'm not even sure if she knows I'm back."

"You should definitely connect with her. I'm sure that would help a lot."

"What about your church?"

Darby flinches. "What do you mean?"

"Surely it provides comfort and answers to the grieving."

"Oh. Um, it isn't really an outreach kind of a church. We aren't trying to save the world or anything like that."

"I thought that's what churches did?"

"Probably some do, but not this one."

"Why not? Isn't that the point?"

She squirms. "We're trying to help each other get to Heaven."

"But not other people?"

"I guess."

"Not even people who are looking for help?"

Darby licks her lips and looks around, color draining from her face. "Why are you asking about all of this?"

"I told you—I need answers. My life doesn't make sense. How can so much bad exist in a world if there's a good creator?"

"That's more than I have time for before Ashley and Emma wake from their nap."

"But we could start."

She sighs.

I hold her gaze. "What's wrong?"

"I'm not really qualified for this."

"For discussing your own religion's beliefs?"

"My heart is the most deceitful thing on earth."

"But if I'm not even part of your group, wouldn't that put you above me?"

Darby clears her throat. "I think I should see you out. I'm going to have to get snacks ready for my girls before they wake up."

"If you can't tell me anything, is there someone else who can?"

She leaps to her feet. "You're already friends with Emmett. Ask him."

"Emmett? He's..." I stumble over my words. "He's part of everything?"

"Yeah. Emmett's practically besties with the top leaders. Let me see you out."

"Okay." I can barely stand on my own two feet.

Emmett didn't give me any indication of being involved, much less being close to the leaders.

Is there anyone I can trust?

One thing is clear.

I need to tell all on my podcast. No more holding back. Regardless of the backlash I receive.

34

Chasing the Forgotten Ones

Murder House Series: Part 4: Fleur Bardot, podcaster

Now that you're all caught up on the background of the case, I have some big news as promised in the subject line of the episode notes.

It's hard to know where to begin. I've learned a lot, and I've debated how much to release and what I should keep to myself while I continue to look into things. But you all are my people, and you're as invested in this as I am.

It's hard to fathom a case where a wife is murdered and her husband is missing, and there has hardly been anything mentioned in the media. That's why I'm here, and some of the things I'm uncovering make this case even more compelling than I ever imagined.

Once you hear what I have to say, you're going to demand justice for Caroline Porter, just as I am. So many details of this case have been completely left out of the minuscule information released.

Those particulars are what makes this case more concerning than ever before.

I know, I know. You want me to get to the point. I'm trying to get there. Really, I am. Like I said, it's hard to know where to start. I suppose I should begin with the murder itself.

The cause of death is still a mystery, even after I've gone into the murder room. I didn't find any obvious signs—there was no blood, no signs of struggle, hardly anything out of place.

However there was one thing about the room that shocked me to my core. Are you ready for this?

First, I need to preface this by saying that a neighbor told me the room was Caroline's craft room.

It most assuredly was not *a craft room. What it was will send a chill down your spine.*

Caroline Porter was killed in her nursery.

Dramatic pause to let the news sink in.

That's right, my friends. Caroline Porter was pregnant. I haven't been able to get my hands on any official documents yet, so I can't confirm this for certain. But given the detail of this room, it's obvious Caroline and Shane were planning on having a baby. If she wasn't pregnant, then maybe they were in the adoption process.

It's impossible to say for now, since as I've already mentioned, the police are so far refusing to talk to me.

That means I need to hear from you, Shane Porter. If you're alive, please *reach out to me. I give you my word—I will not tell anyone where you are. The police aren't helping me, so why should I help them?*

I want to hear your side of the story. Did the killer drag you away and leave you for dead? Were you able to get away from him? Have you been living in fear, hiding all this time?

I've found nothing indicating your guilt. Nothing. I live in your home, and everything I've seen points to a loving husband who wanted nothing but the best for his wife and future child.

Reach out to me, and we can get your side of the story out to the world. You deserve to be heard. To speak and tell everyone what really happened.

Shane, if you are out there—please trust me with your side of the story. Things are coming to light, and together we can prove your innocence. But I can't do that without you. Well, actually I probably could eventually, but it would be a lot easier with your help.

I've been talking with neighbors, friends, and anyone willing tell me anything. I'm picking up little clues here and there. Not to mention things I'm finding around the house. There was even something in your office pointing to my sister. Imagine how I felt when I saw that.

My sister Lourdes was the reason I started this podcast in the first place. Now I've come full circle. I'm back in our hometown and am finding links to her right here in the former Porter house.

Please, Shane, reach out. All of my contacts are in the show notes, or you can use any social media channel. It's up to you. I'll be waiting.

Reach out and we can meet whenever and wherever you pick. We'll lock it in.

Another pause.

Now I'm talking to the people around here who knew Caroline. I'm certain some of you know more than you're saying, and I'm having some trouble understanding why this is. If you're afraid of someone, I'll help protect you. There are ways to go about that outside of the town boundaries.

I'm not afraid of anyone or anything—especially not in the same way many locals are. I was gone for over a decade and got used to the big city. These small town issues don't ruffle my feathers. Let's work together.

Caroline deserves justice. She and her baby *deserve justice*. She was a young mother-to-be with dreams and hopes. The fact that the nursery was put together with such care tells me as much. She wanted this baby, and she should be here right now with her toddler. Maybe with another baby, too.

Instead, now both Caroline and her child are gone. We are the only ones who can do anything for her. I'm not entirely sure why her *case has been shoved under the rug and ignored for so long—though I do have my thoughts, and it involves a certain religious organization—but that stops now.*

Caroline, we will get you and your baby justice. And for the rest of you...

Stay safe and hug your loved ones tightly—you never know when one of you might go missing.

35

Fleur

Saturday, late morning

It's taken every ounce of my self-control not to obsessively check all of my social media, refreshing messages every minute. I have alerts set up. If Shane reaches out, I'll know.

Ever since I published the latest podcast last night, the comments on my online posts have blown up. A couple of them have gone viral.

I'd been right—people are going crazy over the fact that Caroline was pregnant when murdered. As if that isn't a vulnerable enough time in life, the chances of being murdered also increase. That last part should not be, and I'm glad to see the outrage, the cries for justice. Hopefully soon, she'll get it.

Now it's a waiting game.

If Shane is alive and following along, my latest episode has to have caught his attention with my mention of the picture I found of him and Lourdes kissing. Obviously I didn't mention that they were kissing, but Shane will know. He's the one who kept the photo and went to the lengths of hiding it.

Part of me questions the wisdom of mentioning the cult. Surely, people around town are listening to the podcast. I can't imagine them not, since a true crime podcaster has moved from New York into the murder house to solve the crime. They must be dying of curiosity.

Since I released the episode, I've jumped at every little sound. In the wee hours, I swore I heard something outside. I couldn't find anything.

I also can't believe I've been back for a week. On one hand, time has flown and it seems like I just arrived, but on the other hand, it also feels like I never left and have been here all my life.

Time is weird like that, passing in ways that don't make sense. I can imagine how those closest to Caroline feel—likely not much different from how I've felt about Lourdes these last fifteen years. I still have moments when I expect to see her or hear from her.

Especially now that I'm back. She never fully left me, but her presence is much stronger here where she lived, walked, and ruled. Where she should still be, assuming she didn't also want to flee. But nobody will ever know.

There are too many cold cases here, too many missing women. Two is too many. My sister and Caroline, and somehow they're connected.

If it was just the photo, I could pass it off as nothing. But not with the locket that now lives around my neck. It's back with our family as it belongs, but who put it there?

That's what worries me. It wasn't inside the house like the picture.

Anyone could've placed it on the windowsill outside.

I make my way to the front of the house and peek outside.

Every time I look, I expect to see someone messing around—letting the air out of my tires again or some such nonsense.

So far, nothing.

That worries me. Is whoever did that not listening to the podcast?

At least I don't have to worry about trying to break into the cult anymore. There's no way they'd let me in now. The best I can hope for is that some of them will come to me to give me their side, that they'll want to clear their name and get the word out there.

Zorro sits, leaning against my leg. I pet him, and he whines.

"Time to go outside again?" I peek out front, and not seeing anything, take him out there. He loves running around the front yard, and I'm curious to see if any neighbors I can't see from inside are watching the house.

He zips around the grass, as usual.

I pretend to be super interested in a shrub, but I'm really casing the street, looking for people who are spying on me. One dad plays ball with his kids. Another mows his lawn even though it's supposed to rain soon. Nobody's glancing my way. If they are, they're discreet.

I'm about ready to call Zorro when the van catches my attention.

The tires are flat again—but not because the air was let out. Each piece of rubber has multiple gashes. It looks like streamers in places.

Everything disappears around me as I struggle to breathe normally. This can't be happening. But it is.

Once I regain my bearings, I turn to get my pup's attention. My voice catches in my throat.

The words "Go Away!" are scrawled across the garage door in red paint.

A mix of anger and humiliation surge through me.

I find my voice and order Zorro inside.

His eyes widen and his tail droops. He can tell from my tone something is wrong.

Good.

We hurry inside, much to the pleasure of my vandal, I'm sure. I slam and lock the door, and even push a chair under the knob for good measure. I struggle to breathe and can't stop shaking.

Zorro nudges my leg, trying to comfort me. Animals are so much better than people. You'd never see a dog destroy property like that—even if they were capable of such violence.

I stumble over to the couch and collapse onto it. Zorro snuggles me, halfway lying on my lap. He licks my hand as I mindlessly stroke his fur.

It isn't like I didn't think something like this could happen. I just wasn't prepared for how violated it made me feel.

One thing is certain—I'm getting close to the truth. Somebody doesn't want the truth about Caroline's murder coming out, and I'm stepping on that person's toes.

That is good news, even if it sucks for my tires and garage. It isn't like they burned my house down or did anything permanent. Tires and paint are easy enough to buy, though a little more challenging without a car to drive. This will just push me to sell the van like I'd planned, so I can get something more my style.

While I certainly don't appreciate the extra work, I choose to consider this a good thing. It's helping me focus in the right direction. And I think I'll leave the paint up for a little while so everyone can see how petty the person is who did it.

The truth will come out. Sooner than later, if I have my way.

I rub Zorro's ears. "Thanks for the pep talk. I needed that."

He licks my face.

Now that I'm feeling better, I check my phone's notifications. Can hardly believe my eyes.

I have a direct message from Shane Porter.

My hand shakes so hard I nearly drop the phone.

Is the DM real, or someone playing a crueler joke than the one outside?

There's only way to find out.

I press the notification to check the message.

36

Caroline

Before

Emmett's house is nothing like I'd have expected. With all of the doilies and knickknacks showcased on shelves, it looks more like a grandma's home than a bachelor pad. But that's the least of my concerns, considering Alpha and Omega are in my house with Shane.

Nothing will ever be the same, and just because Emmett brought me inside doesn't mean he'll help me. Or want our baby.

He pulls me close, and his heartbeat thunders in my ear. "What happened?"

I gasp for air, not knowing where to begin. "I can't go back home."

"What? Why not?"

"Shane is dangerous!"

"Did he threaten you?" Emmett growls.

"I can't go back home," I repeat, not answering his question. "Ever."

He sighs. "You have to be able to go get your stuff at least."

"I can't."

"You have rights!"

"Shane's an attorney, remember? Not only is he friends with every other lawyer within fifty miles, but he's on a first name basis with every judge in this county. I don't stand a chance."

Emmet steps back and looks into my eyes. "You still have rights. He can't block you from what's yours."

"You've clearly never dealt with the court system before."

Or the church leadership, but I don't mention them. There's no point.

He frowns. "You don't need to make any decisions right now. Come sit down. Are you hungry or thirsty?"

"Yes to both."

"I'll fix that." Emmett heads to the kitchen. I follow then collapse into a seat at the table. He goes through cabinets and the fridge, pulling out various things.

I play with the edge of the tablecloth, which is clearly made by hand. "Are you housesitting for an old lady?"

He laughs. "It's my parents' house, and I keep it up for them. Mom inherited my grandma's things."

"That explains it. This place isn't exactly giving off 'single guy' vibes."

"Now you know the real reason I haven't had you in here." He winks at me before setting a glass of sparkling water in front of me. "Hopefully you don't mind reheated casserole. Dorothy next door makes me at least two a week. Says she worries about me."

My stomach growls at the thought of warm food. "That sounds great. I wish someone would cook for me."

Emmett throws me a questioning glance as he piles casserole onto two plates. "Shane never cooks?"

"He's too busy with important work. He's bringing justice to people who have been denied their rights."

"That's no excuse."

I shrug. "He can't help it. He works a lot."

"Don't defend him!" Emmett's nostrils flare as he puts one of the plates in the microwave.

"It's true," I insist. "He's busy helping people who need it."

"He doesn't have to make you do everything around the house."

"He grew up as a foster kid. What else could he know?"

Emmett crosses his arms. "Anyone can decide to be a decent human being."

"It doesn't matter anymore because I'm getting away from everything."

The microwave dings, and he takes out the plate. "Do you know where you're going?"

"Not yet."

He sets the plate in front of me then puts the other one in the microwave. "Back to my point of you needing to get back in the house. I didn't see your car out front. Does he have that too?"

"I don't have it anymore."

"So, he's leaving you with *nothing*?" Emmett's practically shouting now.

"I'm walking away. He isn't kicking me out."

"Is he keeping you from returning to gather your things?"

My only response is to start eating. I'm so famished, I inhale the food, not caring that it burns my mouth.

Emmett sits next to me with his plate, and we eat in silence.

I get up and warm myself another plate. Luckily, there's plenty. If this is how much food Dorothy makes him regularly, Emmett probably doesn't ever have to cook for himself.

After we're both done, I take our plates and start washing.

"What do you think you're doing?" he demands.

"Cleaning the plates."

"You aren't my servant. Sit back down and let me do that."

I hardly know what to do with a man who wants to help out with domestic duties, but I let him.

Once he's done, we go to the living room where he covers me with a quilt. "Rest here. I'll be right back, then we'll figure out your next steps. There has to be a way to put Shane in his place."

All I can do is shake my head. I'm married to a powerful attorney—there's nothing anyone can do to help me. The best I can hope for is to make a clean break.

When Emmett returns, he hands me a single red rose.

"Where'd you get that?"

"It's the last one from the garden out back. I thought it might cheer you up."

I breathe in its sweet fragrance. "It's perfect."

He sits next to me and wraps an arm around my shoulder. Maybe somehow everything will be okay, as improbable as that seems.

Knock, knock!

My entire body freezes. "Who's that?"

Emmett gives me a squeeze. "I'll check. You stay here."

I nod, shivering.

Knock, knock! Knock, knock!

He gets up and hurries over to the door. Peeks out the peephole.

I'm ready to run if I have to.

Emmett rushes over to me. "It's Alpha and Omega. Also a few other guys from the leadership team."

Terror charges through every inch of me. I have to get out of here. Emmett and I don't stand a chance against that many people.

Knock, knock! Knock, knock! Knock, knock!

"Quick—follow me!" Emmett pulls me up then leads me

through a hallway similar to mine into a back bedroom. "Stay in here."

He slams the door. Something clicks.

A lock?

Is he trapping me in here?

His footsteps thunder away.

I reach for the knob, fumbling in the dark room.

Locked.

The floor seems to disappear from underneath me.

I twist the knob again and again. Still locked. I feel around for a light switch. Find it.

Unfortunately, only dim light illuminates the room. But it's more than enough.

The sight before me is far more frightening than facing the church leaders. This room is the stuff horror films are made of—knives hanging on racks, chains, brown stains splattered all over the walls. The bed frame and mattress have similar discoloration.

What has happened in here? And what is he planning on doing with me?

How could I have ever trusted him? This is the last place I should've come for help.

Must get away.

I drop the rose and pull on the doorknob with all my might.

It doesn't budge. I run around the various torture devices to the curtains, push them aside.

The window is boarded up from the outside. There isn't a bathroom attached to the room.

I'm trapped.

My only hope is to scream. How the tides have turned now that I want Shane or the church leaders to save me when I came here to avoid them.

I try to take deep breaths but can only manage shallow ones. It'll have to be good enough.

If I want to live.

I pound on the door and scream as loudly as I can. Keep it up until both my throat and fists are raw.

Nobody comes.

My only option is getting out of here on my own. I need to escape all of them. Have to protect my baby and get us to safety.

I throw myself against the door. Then I kick it. Repeat the process.

It doesn't so much as buckle or crack.

There has to be a way out of here.

Someone knocks on the other side. Emmett's voice sounds. "You aren't doing much to keep from being noticed by them."

"Let me out of here, you psychopath!"

"I see you turned the lights on."

"Open the door!" I pound some more, not caring how much it hurts.

"You may as well make yourself comfortable," he says. "You're going to be in there a long, long time."

"Get me out!" I throw myself against the door again.

"Stop now, or you're going to regret it!"

"I don't care! You're crazy!" I kick the door several times.

"Do what you want—you'll eventually tire yourself out. All the easier for me. But you're never getting out of there. Not alive, anyway."

Tears blur my vision. I scream, kick, and punch the door until I collapse.

The rose is next to me. I hold onto it, the only other form of life in this room outside of me.

If what Emmett said is true, then it will outlast me and the baby I will now probably never meet.

I sob until I fall asleep.

37

Fleur

Saturday, late morning

Just as I'm about to tap the notification to read Shane's message—

Ding-dong!

What timing.

I grumble as I make my way to the door, Zorro rushing ahead of me, barking and wagging his tail.

Hopefully this is just a package I need to sign for, or better yet, someone with a brand new set of tires.

When I glance out, it's Emmett. What could he possibly want that's so urgent he can't send a simple text?

I throw open the door and force a neighborly smile. "What's up?"

He glances around. "Can I come in?"

Zorro runs circles around him before darting to the front yard.

"I thought we'd established that's a no."

"But I'm no longer a stranger."

"True, but I have things to do. What do you need?"

His mouth curls in annoyance. "I was able to talk with someone in the Beacon of Truth Fellowship."

"You have my interest."

"Can I come in?" He glances behind me.

"Still no."

"Don't you want to know what they said?"

"Can't you tell me from the porch?" I step outside, closing the door behind me. "I'm all ears."

"Fine. But there's no reason for you not to trust me."

"Call me overcautious." I sit at the porch swing and look at him expectantly. "What did the church people say?"

"The higher ups are willing to talk to you." He sits next to me, not leaving much room between us.

"What's the catch?" I try to scoot away but he doesn't get the clue.

"No catch."

"Then why are you here? This is something that could be said over text."

"They're willing to talk with you about Caroline and Shane, but only if I'm there. I'll be a mediator of sorts. You know, an unbiased party."

"Why would there need to be a mediator? This isn't court."

"They're... shall we say, nervous."

"About talking to me?"

Emmett nods. "You're basically a reporter. You could spin what they say in ways to make them look bad. If I'm there, I'm a witness to what was really said."

I roll my eyes so hard they practically fly across the street. "Seriously?"

"Yes."

"All I want is answers—something nobody seems to want to

hand out. I've dealt with closed off people before, but this case is in a league of its own."

"And now you have the opportunity to speak with them."

"With you there as my babysitter."

"Mediator."

"Whatever."

"What do you say?" He looks at me expectantly.

"I'll think about it."

His brows draw together for the briefest moment. "They need an answer—and you need an in. What's to think about?"

"If I do this interview, it's on *my* terms. I'm not meeting in some creepy building or away from public spaces."

"They aren't going to talk if other people are around. I'll keep you safe."

I resist the urge to roll my eyes again. "Thanks for the offer, but I'll get back to you. If they aren't willing to wait, then that's my answer."

He frowns. "You're sure?"

"Yes. I'm not going to be bullied."

"Nobody's bullying you."

"I'll be the judge of that."

"Do you know when you might have your answer?"

"Soon."

"That's pretty vague." He stares at me. "Especially for someone so desperate for answers."

"Desperate?"

He shrugs. "Not a judgment. It just is what it is."

"I'm looking for answers. You're mistaken if you take that for desperation."

"I wasn't trying to offend you."

"Then you should go."

"I'm not ready to."

"Well, I need to get back inside." I rise and call for Zorro, who hurries over to me. "I'll let you know when I've made my decision."

"Don't wait too long."

"You aren't going to force my hand. I'll decide when I'm ready."

He mumbles something, and all I can make out is the word woman.

"Tell me you didn't just say something misogynistic."

"Of course not."

"I'll be in touch."

"Great." He doesn't get up.

I take Zorro inside and lock the knob and deadbolt. Emmett can wait outside as long as he wants. I'm not going to be pressured by anyone, much less some cult leaders.

Now I can finally check out the message from Shane and see if it's legit.

Did I convince him to come out of hiding? I try to keep my hopes low, as I know how rampant trolls are online. Some people have nothing better to do than mess with people who are trying to do good in the world.

It takes me a moment to brush off the interaction with Emmett. I hadn't taken him to be someone so pushy, but whatever. It just makes me glad I haven't allowed myself to be alone with him.

There's something about him that hasn't sat right with me since our first meeting. I just can't put my finger on what that is. I'm not sure I care enough to find out, either. It might be time to start avoiding him for my own wellbeing.

Once I settle on the couch, I find the notification and tap it.

My heart races as it loads. It seems to take forever.

The message shows the profile picture of a handsome picture of Shane at a party, based on the background. Curious, I click to look at his profile.

As expected, no posts in the last two years. I scroll through, checking out pictures of him with Caroline, him with friends, pictures of his beloved car, and other similar posts. It isn't my first time checking out his social media presence, but now that he's sent me a message, it shows me more.

Wait, no. It isn't because he sent me the DM. We now have a mutual friend, so more of his posts show. I don't bother to see who we have in common. I've added several locals in attempt to contact people.

I hurry through the feed, checking for anything telling. Not that I expect him to post that he'd killed anyone, but maybe he'd hinted at problems in paradise.

Nothing. Just typical posts from a married dude, showing off the fruits of his labor. Clearly he was in love with his car. More than Caroline, if the number of posts tells any sort of story.

I think it does.

Even though nothing points to the answers I want—so desperately, according to Emmett—Shane's profile does tell me one thing.

He's legit. This is his actual profile. It hasn't been faked.

Not to say someone couldn't have hacked into it. If someone was hungry enough for attention, they could figure out a way.

Time to read that DM.

My hand shakes as I tap my way back to it. It's a fairly short message:

Fleur,

I've been able to listen to your podcast episodes. I can't tell you how grateful I am that you believe in me. All this time I've been locked away—held captive against my will—but after hearing that jerk play the podcast episodes on repeat, I found my lost strength. I managed to get out, and I'm using a library computer to log into my old account. I'm sure those dirty cops are watching and know I'm out. They're involved in this!

I hope you're serious about letting me tell my story. The world needs to know the truth. I didn't do that horrible crime, I swear. Whatever you do, don't trust anyone in the Beacon of Truth Fellowship or the cops.

Shane

I read it over several times, trying to make sense of it. Who held him captive? Why didn't he tell me their name? Does he not know? Where is he now?

The questions fly through my mind faster than I can keep up with. But there's only way I can get answers.

I tap to reply. My fingers shake as I tap out the message.

Shane,

Thank you for reaching out. I would love to meet with you and hear everything. I'm sure I can help you.

Since you're logging in from the library, I don't know when you'll see this, but I'll keep my phone on me and get any message you send right away.

Name the time and place, and I'll be there.

Fleur

Heart practically in my throat, I tap send. I take a deep breath. Shane Porter is actually alive—and innocent if he's to be believed.

Now it's a waiting game. I turn up the volume on my phone as high as it will go. He could text me anytime, though it will probably be a while.

I'm about to tap away from the app when something catches my eye.

Dancing dots.

Shane's replying now. He must've been waiting at the library.

Either that, or he's lying about everything and like me, he's messaging with his phone.

Not that it matters. Just like I told Emmett, I'm not meeting anyone alone.

Shane's message comes through. He suggests meeting at a

park not far away. It has benches spaced far apart and away from the playground. It's public and allows for private conversation.

It's perfect.

We go back and forth several times, agreeing to meet as soon as we can both get there.

38

Fleur

Saturday, early afternoon

As I fly out of the house, I barely notice Emmett still sitting on the swing as I lock the door.

"Decide already?" he asks.

"I'm not talking with them."

"What?" His mouth forms a straight line. "But you need them if you want answers."

"Turns out I don't."

"That's not possible."

"Actually it is." I race to the van.

It has no usable tires. This can't be happening.

"Something wrong?" Emmett appears at my side.

"Nope." I hurry down the sidewalk and pull out my phone.

"Where are you going?"

I ignore him as I tap what I need to set up a ride.

"Do you need me to drive you somewhere?" he asks. "I'd be more than happy to."

A cold chill runs down my spine. He *wants* to give me a ride? Plus, he's so eager to mediate between the cult leaders and me.

Emmett must be the one behind my slashed tires. It's the only explanation.

I keep my expression steady so as not to alert him to my revelation.

"Slow down!" he calls.

Apparently I've started running and didn't notice. I don't change my pace.

"Fleur! Let me help you!"

My heart hammers furiously, probably from both the running and being so close to someone dangerous. If there are as many cult members in this neighborhood as I think, I can't call out for help.

They haven't trusted me since I moved in, and now I've called them out on my podcast.

I'm in this alone until I can get into my ride. The app shows me what car to look for and where. I'll barely make it if I keep this pace.

Emmett catches up to me. "What are you looking at?"

"Nothing that concerns you." I gasp for air. "You can go back to your home."

"I don't want to."

"And I don't want you running with me."

"It's a free country."

"What's your problem?"

"I don't have one."

Liar. I don't respond. Need to conserve my energy. In fact, I slow a little so I can speed up when I get closer to the meeting spot.

"Are you afraid of me?" Emmett asks.

"I'm not scared of anything."

"You should be."

My blood runs cold. I never should have spoken with him, much less had lunch with him.

Too late for that now.

"I'd like you to leave me alone."

"This is public ground."

At least I'm getting close to the meeting spot. And as he pointed out, this is public space. He won't be able to do anything without either being seen by someone or caught by a camera somewhere.

A red car starts to pull up to the curb.

I think that's my ride. I'm feeling too frantic to remember all the details, but I'm pretty sure it was red. I don't let on that the car interests me.

Emmett keeps talking, which is to my advantage. He's distracting himself, and if I don't listen to him, I can almost hear my own thoughts.

I pull out my phone and glance at from an angle he hopefully can't see.

He doesn't seem to notice.

The car is a match.

Relief washes through me, though I'm not out of the woods yet.

When I get to the car, the driver rolls down the window and we both confirm our details. I can't get into the back fast enough.

"Is that guy with you?" she asks.

Emmett's reaching for the door.

"No. Go!"

She hits the gas hard enough it whips my head back.

"Thanks."

"Is he stalking you? Do you want me to report him?"

Not that the police would likely do anything, given how they already hate me for looking into Caroline's case.

"No, but thanks."

"Think about it."

Luckily, she isn't one for small talk so I'm able to think about what I'll say to Shane when I see him. I can hardly believe I'm about to see him, that he actually reached out because of my podcast. It seems surreal, especially after dealing with Emmett following me down the street.

"We're here." She's pulls up to the curb next to the park, and gives me a spiel about rating her. I thank her, toss her a cash tip, and get out of the car, looking for Shane.

After all of that, he better be here.

I hurry past the playground and toward the woods.

There are several benches that can barely be seen from here. He must be at one of those.

With my sights focused ahead, I race past the kids playing and through the grass which needs to be mowed. Water soaks my shoes as I make my way through the field.

The benches within sight are empty.

Maybe he hasn't had time to make it here yet. If his story is true about being locked away against his will all this time, he doesn't have a car, either—and he probably doesn't have a phone to order a ride. He has nothing.

I make my way to the farthest bench, tucked away so close to the trees it's nearly invisible.

A man sits on it, his face blocked by a branch.

That must be him.

My knees turn to rubber. Am I ready for this? Will I remember all my questions.

There's only one way to find out.

I march toward him.

39

Fleur

Saturday, early afternoon

My feet soak in more water as I stand, staring at the figure in front of me.

He rises and waves me over. It has to be him.

I can hardly believe my eyes. The entire reason I moved into the house—I drew him out. He's going to tell me the truth that I can't get from anyone else.

Shane waves again, and I make myself step toward him. My legs feel weighted down.

Finally, I stumble to him. Stop when he's just beyond my reach.

It's definitely him, but he looks so different. Older, for starters. If he's been through such a traumatic ordeal, that makes sense. But isn't just that—he's super skinny, with sunken cheeks and his clothes barely hang onto him, like he's a skeleton underneath. He also has bruises and scars.

This is a man who has been through hell. My heart aches for him.

He stares at me, as if taking me in as much as I'm taking him in.

I clear my throat. "Do you need anything? I didn't think to bring food."

"No, I'm fine."

"You don't *look* fine."

"I am." Shane seems to want to say more. He also looks like he could crumble into a pile of dust at any moment. "You want to talk?"

I nod, struggling to find my voice.

He sits on the bench, leaving me plenty of room to sit where I want—unlike Emmett who forced himself right next to me.

I shudder at the thought.

"Are you okay?" Shane asks.

"*You're* concerned about me?"

He gives me a sad smile. "You look like you've seen a ghost."

I feel like I'm looking at one, but I don't tell him that. Instead, I collapse onto the bench, leaving a comfortable distance between us. "Are *you* okay?"

"I'm free. What more could I ask for?"

"A lot."

He doesn't disagree.

My mind spins with a hundred different questions. It's hard to know where to start. I can't believe I'm sitting next to him. My podcast worked. It actually brought him to me.

"So, you moved into my house?"

"Technically it's my house now." A small smile tugs on my lips. "But yes, I did."

"That must be weird."

"You have no idea."

"Oh, I can imagine." He looks deep in thought for a

moment. "It isn't a murder house, though. I hate to break it to you."

I stare at him in disbelief. "What?"

"He didn't murder her there. It was all staged."

"That explains why I couldn't see any signs."

Shane nods, his expression pained. "I tried to save her, but I was too late. They moved her body to our house to frame me."

"He? They? How many people are involved in this?"

"Three." He pinches the bridge of his nose. "More, if you consider all the people involved in the coverup."

"Including the police?"

"Especially them."

"Who are they?"

Shane takes a deep breath and buries his face in his palms.

"You don't have to talk about anything you don't want to."

He looks at me with an intensity in his tear-rimmed eyes. "It isn't that." His voice cracks. "I've been having a hard time adjusting to life on the outside. I was in that room for two years."

"I can't even imagine."

Shane clears his throat. "I had to look at Caroline's dried blood every single day. They didn't even let me say goodbye. After I failed at protecting her, they locked me in the room and took her away. Said if I ever got out, everyone would blame me and I'd go to jail. But honestly, prison would've been an improvement."

"That sounds like a nightmare. Worse, actually."

"It was torture. He only fed me a few times a week and beat me first. I fought back, obviously, but after not eating for two or three days I didn't exactly have the upper hand."

I don't even know what to say. "How did you get out?"

"He's been distracted lately. I think it must've started around the time you moved in. I managed to get in a good right hook, and it threw him off. I ran right out of the house and didn't stop until I was safely away."

"You must need something, despite what you told me."

"Like a place to live?"

I start to say something, but he suddenly turns his attention something behind me.

"Don't trust him." Shane's tone holds an edge. "Everything he says is a lie."

I whip around.

Emmett. How did he know to find me here? He couldn't have followed the car while on foot.

My stomach sinks. The cult—they're everywhere in this town. My driver must've told him. She has to be in on it. That's the only explanation.

"I'm sorry. I didn't mean to, but I led him right here."

"You couldn't have known." Shane keeps his gaze on Emmett though talking to me. "So much has changed since you left town."

"Clearly."

He rises and stands between me and Emmett, who is rapidly approaching us. If he thinks he can protect me in his condition, he's sadly mistaken. At least it's two against one if Emmett decides to do something stupid.

The look in his eyes tells me he may very well do just that.

I step around Shane. "What do you want?"

"Don't listen to him. He's delusional—not to mention a wife killer."

Shane lunges toward him.

I put my hand out. "Don't let him get to you."

"He's accusing me of the murder *he* committed! I would never have hurt Caroline!"

"Then let's do an interview for the podcast. Tell your story that way. Hurting him won't do anything for your cause."

The two stare each other down.

Emmett steps forward, keeping his attention on Shane. "We don't need to involve her. Why don't we step aside and handle this like men?"

I balk. "What is this—the eighteen hundreds? You think you're John Wayne or something?"

He waves me off.

"Could you be any more misogynistic?"

Emmett turns to me. "Do you think you could stop talking for just two seconds?"

"That's cute coming from the guy who never shuts up."

He balls his fist and holds it up. "Learn your place."

"Learn *yours*."

Emmett turns to Shane. "Sure you want to work with her? She's about as un-submissive as they come."

"Thank you," I quip.

Shane turns to me. "He's the one who killed Caroline. The top church leaders held me down and tried to make me watch, but I closed my eyes. I fought against them trying to save Caroline, obviously, but Omega gave me this." He points to a scar on the side of his neck. "They both walked away with injuries as well. I didn't have a weapon, as I didn't expect them to turn on me. Do yourself a favor and don't trust anyone in the Beacon of Truth Fellowship."

My mind reels. Emmett murdered Caroline, and he kept trying to get inside my house.

Was he planning on killing me too? That's the only explanation, since I came specifically to solve the crime.

He also said he was going to be a mediator so I could talk to the church leaders.

Everything out of his mouth had to have been a lie. He made it sound like he wasn't involved with the group.

It's a good thing I've never trusted strangers since Lourdes disappeared. How tragically ironic that her death very well could have saved my life.

Emmett whips out an enormous knife. Its blade is nearly as long as his forearm. He glowers at me. "If you go now, I'll leave you alone. This is between him and me."

"Man to man?" I square my shoulders.

"Exactly."

I don't budge.

Shane inches closer to me.

Emmett's nostrils flare as he aims his weapon at me. "I don't *want* to hurt a woman, but I will."

"Obviously. You killed Caroline."

"She left me no choice."

Shane steps toward him. "You didn't have to kill her!" His voice cracks. "She didn't deserve that!"

"She did, actually. She was pregnant with my baby."

My mouth falls open. "*You* were the father?"

All the pieces fall into place. Everyone has been looking in the wrong direction—she had a lover and he killed her.

Once again, the statistics are right.

Emmett leaps toward Shane, swinging his knife.

40

Fleur

Saturday, early afternoon

There's no time to think—I only react by slamming myself into Emmett. The blade barely misses slicing across Shane's face.

Emmett drops the knife as he sails sideways and falls.

I stumble, nearly crashing onto the ground.

Shane reaches for me. Steadies me.

"Grab the knife!" I point to it, just a few feet from him. Halfway between him and Emmett.

He steps toward it, reaches down.

Emmett scrambles over at the same time.

They're both equally close to grabbing it.

I gasp, frozen for a split second, but then I lunge forward too.

Shane and Emmett collide, neither reaching the blade. Emmett punches Shane, who wraps his fingers around Emmett's neck. They crash to the damp grass then roll around.

The knife is *under* them.

I can't reach it without getting kicked, hit, or pinned. Not that it stops me from racing over. Trying to figure out a way to grab it.

Their arms and legs swing wildly, making it impossible for me to get close enough to reach the knife. Maybe if I had a long branch.

I spin, study the tree line. None lie on the ground. Most of the trees have high branches, but maybe I can find a low one, break it off. I glance back at the two guys. They're still wrestling. No way for me to get near the knife.

One of them cries out, another grunts. I need to do something to help Shane. He's already in a weakened state. I race to the edge of the forest, search for a branch I can reach. There are a few within my grasp if I jumped. Not sure if I could break them off.

There's only one way to find out. I run, crouch, leap. Sail through the air.

My fingertips brush the bark. I land, no joy.

Need to go higher. I try again, concentrating harder. Spring up. My palms brush the branch. I close my fingers, wrap them around it. Dangle in the air. I did it!

I swing and sway, trying to put enough pressure on it to break off it.

Behind me, Shane and Emmett are making louder noises.

Must break this branch. I swing and wiggle with as much effort as I can manage.

Not even a crack, nothing.

One of the guys cries out in pain. Sounds like Shane.

My fingers slip. I squeeze harder. Bark digs into my skin. My grip lessens.

I slide. Try to hang on.

Fail. Fall.

Crash to the ground.

No!

The fight grows louder. Now they're standing, grappling.

They've moved away from the knife. I can grab it and threaten Emmett.

I race over, pick up the weapon. "Hey, Emmett. Look what I have!"

Both of them look my way.

Relief floods Shane's face.

Emmett's brows draw together. "Hand it over."

I step toward them, aiming the blade at him. "Let Shane go."

He glances between Shane and me. "Don't do something you'll regret, princess."

"Princess? Who are you calling princess?"

Shane looks slightly amused.

"Look, we all know you don't want to get in the middle of men's business."

I pounce, land next to him. Press the knife to the bottom of his neck. "Want to say that again? Or maybe you'd prefer getting killed by a woman?"

He backs up. "You won't hurt me, little miss."

"No?" I slice the blade down his arm. Blood trickles from the long cut.

Emmett makes a high-pitched squeal as he covers part of the wound with his other hand. "How dare you?"

"I don't know what your problem is, but you don't have the right to take people's lives or boss them around. When I thought we were becoming friends, I didn't take you for a misogynist."

"You never did pay any attention to me. Worked out in my favor this time."

"What?"

He glares at me. "You and your sister were always so stuck up, so focused on yourselves that you never noticed the nice people. You were only ever interested in the jerks. Why do women always want *them*?"

"I seriously have no idea what you're talking about."

Emmett's eyes narrow to tiny slits. "You don't even remember me from school, do you?"

I study him. "Sorry, no."

"I was a freshman when you were a senior. You and your snobbish friend Mia thought you were better than literally everyone. I thought now that we're all adults, things would be different."

I struggle to remember him, but can't. What senior girl pays any attention to the freshman boys? Most of us were trying to get the attention of college guys. But it won't do any good to tell him that. "Mia isn't a snob, and neither of us had any intention of hurting anyone. I apologize if that's what happened. She would too, if she was here."

He snorts. "*If* that's what happened?"

"It took me years to work through the pain of what happened to Lourdes. Any slight I gave you wasn't on purpose. I always tried to be nice to everyone, but it was impossible to give everyone attention."

"Especially a lowly freshman."

"It wasn't like that."

"What was it like, then?" He glares at me.

Shane steps between us. "As fascinating as this is, what does it have to do with anything? I thought we were here because of Caroline, not Fleur."

Emmett scoffs. "You don't know anything, pretty boy. Neither of you do. Both of you skate through life with your good looks. Life is easy for you people. You don't know what it's like for the rest of us—the ones people don't treat like royalty."

"My life is *easy*?" Shane yells. "You tortured me for *two years*. Not only did you steal my wife from me, but you took a significant portion of my life from me!"

"Now you're on the same level as the rest of us. Poor baby." He gives me a mocking expression.

I hand the knife to Shane. "Take care of him, while I call the cops."

Something I should've done before trying to break branches, but I can't change that. It's impossible to think straight right now.

Emmett leaps back. "I'm not going to jail."

"That's what you think." I dial 911 and press call.

"You don't get it. Alpha and Omega *own* the police department. Everyone in there works for them. They won't let me go down!"

I shrug. "Then stick around. Prove me wrong."

Shane grabs his arm, and shoves the knife toward his throat. Emmett punches him, and Shane stumbles back, letting go of Emmett.

Someone answers my call.

Just as Emmett runs and disappears into the woods.

Shane chases after him.

I explain the situation—where we are, what happened, and what Emmett looks like and is wearing. It's amazing the clarity of mind I have now compared to a few minutes ago.

The operator tries to keep me on the phone, but there's no point.

Emmett is long gone. Given the state Shane is in, he won't be able to keep up. If the cult has as much control over everything as it appears, Emmett won't face charges unless an agency with more power takes over the case.

I run into the woods. After a few minutes, I find Shane walking toward me.

He shakes his head. "Emmett got away. I'm too weak to keep up."

"At least you're safe. That's all that really matters. I can't believe you were in his house the whole time."

"He soundproofed the room. I screamed at the top of my lungs for days. Nobody ever heard me. I finally stopped to conserve my energy. He didn't give me enough food to waste my efforts like that." Shane stops walking only an inch from me.

Our gazes lock, and with the dimness of the woods he looks almost the same as he did in high school.

I brush a scar under his eye with my fingertip. "What did he do to you?"

Shane blinks slowly. "I don't want to talk about it."

"I'm sorry." I frown. "I can't even imagine."

He rests his hand over mine. "I'm glad you can't. It was a nightmare."

My breath catches.

Shane closes the distance between us and presses his lips on mine. It has all the magic of a first kiss all over again, while at the same time also feeling like all the time spent apart never happened. As if we'd always been together, like I'd never made the mistake of running away. I've missed this so much.

I pull away, short of breath.

He swallows, his Adam's apple especially noticeable with his low weight. "I can't believe you're back here. In my house, no less."

"I had to find out what happened to you. Everyone had their theories, but I didn't believe any of them—not that you'd run and hidden, not that you'd killed your wife."

"Never."

Silence rests between us, his hand still on mine, which is on his face.

I find my voice. "I saw the picture of you and Lourdes kissing."

"What picture?"

"In your office drawer. Do you still love her?"

His eyes soften. "I never did. You should know that." He looks hurt.

"Why keep the photo?"

"I didn't."

"What do you mean? I found it."

"I never knew a photo like that existed. It's like I always told you—she and I were together only because it made sense. Everyone wanted to see the homecoming king and queen together in real life. That's all it ever was."

"But—"

"Nothing." His eyes hold an intensity to them. "It was always only ever you."

"But Caroline…"

"I married her because you ran off to New York and made it clear you were never returning, that it was too painful."

"Didn't you love her?"

"Of course, but she never could replace you. The heart wants what it wants."

My mouth gapes.

"And I knew you felt the same way when you said what you did on your podcast. I knew I had to fight for us."

"When I mentioned the locket."

His mouth curves up. "When you said we would 'lock it in' it could only mean one thing. You want to be with me as much I want to be with you."

I breathe a sigh of relief. "I knew you'd get the secret message."

"Obviously."

Sirens sound in the distance, growing louder, closer.

"We need to get you to the ambulance. After what you've been through, you need medical attention."

"All I want is you." He kisses me deeply, making my heart soar far above the treetops.

"First, let them look you over. I'm worried about you." I thread my fingers through his and drag him out of the woods.

An ambulance sits near the playground.

Perfect. Shane and I can fully reconnect once he's recovered from his ordeal. And now that Caroline's murder is solved, I can walk away from all of this. Announce Emmett's guilt to my podcast and move on with my life. But I can't leave it at this.

I turn to Shane. "You'll help me find Emmett, right?"

"Of course. He needs to pay for what he's done to me and Caroline, and if the police won't do anything—I sure will."

41

Chasing the Forgotten Ones

Murder House Series: Part 7: Fleur Bardot, podcaster

This week has been a whirlwind—as I'm sure you all have noticed. This is my seventh podcast in as many days! The things that have happened today alone would take hours to explain, so this is going to be a highlight reel of sorts, to give you an idea of what's coming. I don't have the time to go in depth on anything, and I'm sure you'll understand momentarily.

It's hard to know where to start with so many revelations, but I'll start with the fact that Shane Porter was not the only man in Caroline's life.

Dramatic Pause.

That's right. Now we have not one but two men who stand as obvious suspects.

I know which of them killed her.

Another Dramatic Pause.

How do I know? Because I heard it from his own mouth.

You heard me right. A confession.

I do have a problem, though. I wasn't able to record the confession.

And there's another issue. He got away.

Obviously, that's a devastating blow.

But there is good news in this mess—Shane Porter, Caroline's husband, is innocent. He came to me, and he wants to talk. I'm not going to say more for now. You'll have to wait for the interview. I want you hear what he has to say in his own words.

That will have to wait until he gets out of the hospital. He's endured a terrible ordeal that nobody should ever have to suffer. Thankfully, he's doing really well considering everything. But I'm going to give him the space to heal and breathe before subjecting him to an interview.

It's coming—don't worry about that. We'll just have to wait.

Another surprise in this case is that the other man is the father of Caroline's baby. Perhaps that doesn't come as a surprise to you true crime fans, given the other guy admitted to killing her.

There's also that cult thrown into the mix, though I'm not really sure how deep their involvement runs. I have a lot of work ahead of me—and it will likely be some time before we get all the answers we're looking for.

Answers are coming. Rest assured, I'm not going to stop until everyone who played a part in this is exposed. I've already been warned this could put my personal safety on the line, but I'm not about to let that stop me. Someone has already gone into my backyard, slashed my tires, and painted a message on my garage door in blood red paint telling me to go away. If they do more, I'll let you know.

Everything will come into the light.

I'm thrilled to at least know who the murderer is—that was why I moved here and started this podcast series. What I didn't realize was answering that question was only the beginning.

Especially with the murderer on the loose. The cult knows who he is. That's all I'm going to say about that.

I wish I could give you more details, but it will all come in time. For now, I'm going to check in on Shane and see about tying up some other loose ends. If I don't have a small update for you tomorrow, then expect a big one soon! I can't wait for Shane to be able to share his story with the world.

Until next time, stay safe and hug your loved ones tightly—you never know when one of you might go missing.

42

The Watcher

Reeling

Everything is a mess. All the effort I put into getting Fleur to come back to town was for nothing.

She kissed Shane.

Shane!

What does that loser have that I don't? And now she lives in *his* house. His! What are the chances he won't return home?

Zero, that's what they are.

Those two are going to be living under the same roof now. All because of me. This is my doing. I have nobody to blame except myself.

Though I never could've seen this coming. Not in a million years.

When did they ever fall in love? This is crazy.

He was her sister's boyfriend. Does that mean she went behind Lourdes's back in high school? Or was it a classic case of them seeking comfort in one another, only to have one thing lead to another?

Regardless, I would've noticed.

I never stopped watching either Bardot sister. I vowed one of them would be mine one day. Now that there is only one, it leaves me no choice. It has to be Fleur.

She and Shane cannot reconnect. Sure, they already kissed. And watching that was a nightmare and a half. I couldn't tear my gaze from them. It was like staring at an accident on the side of the road. It wasn't because I wanted to witness it, but I couldn't look away.

That was one wrench I didn't plan for. How could I have?

Does that mean Fleur thought Shane left the locket for her to find? She must have mistakenly thought he had it.

He didn't. It was me. Me! I had it.

Lourdes was enraged when she realized she'd *lost* it. She accused all her friends of taking it. If people hadn't been so scared of her, they would've told her how crazy she was acting. I could see it in everyone's eyes—that was exactly what they were thinking.

It made me feel so powerful to have that much control over the queen bee. All I had to do was take a stupid necklace, then she went off the deep end. Apparently it was a family heirloom or some nostalgic garbage like that.

Whatever. I could've given it back to her, but then the necklace became a symbol of the strength I had. It was something nobody ever saw in me.

But it was there. I knew it, and that stupid little heart locket reminded me every day.

It wasn't until I lured Fleur back home that I was willing to part with it.

Now, seeing that ugly white minivan parked in her driveway was my new symbol. I'd singlehandedly brought her across the country. She left a fiancé and her entire life behind.

Because of me. If that isn't power, I don't know what is.

It's glorious. Now to harness that to win my woman.

She's mine—she just doesn't know it yet.

Once I have her, then I'll be able to focus on my real goal.

Taking over the Beacon of Truth Fellowship. Knocking Alpha and Omega down about twenty pegs. Better yet, making them disappear altogether.

It'll be trickier now. Everyone is on edge after that latest podcast episode. Fleur didn't mention our church by name, but it's more than obvious who she was talking about when she referred to the cult.

Fleur was right about one thing—she's in far more danger now than she was before.

READ SECRETS WE HIDE to continue the saga today!

BOOKS BY STACY CLAFLIN

For a printable checklist of the books:

https://stacyclaflin.com/reading-list/

PSYCHOLOGICAL THRILLERS

Brannon House

The Perfect Death

Family Secrets

The Darkest Garden

Shattered Pieces

Grave Memories

Drowning Silence

The Watcher

Her Last Breath

Secrets We Hide

Ariana Jones

Watch Your Back

Don't Look Now

Without a Trace

Never Letting Go

Lie in Wait

No Way Out

Alex Mercer Thrillers

Girl in Trouble

Turn Back Time

Little Lies

Against All Odds

Don't Forget Me

Tainted Love

Take On Me

Danger Zone

Lady in Red

White Wedding

Careless Whisper

Never Surrender

The Gone Saga

The Gone Trilogy: Gone, Held, Over

Dean's List

No Return

Recluse Island

The Hotel's Secret

The Father's Secret

The Corpse's Secret

Thriller Standalones

Don't Trust Her

Lies Never Sleep

Lost and Found

EMOTIONAL ROMANCE

Flawed Souls

When Tomorrow Starts Without Me

The Only Things You Can Take

When You Start to Miss Me

FAMILY SAGA ROMANCE

The Hunters

Seaside Surprises

Seaside Heartbeats

Seaside Dances

Seaside Kisses

Seaside Christmas

Bayside Wishes

Bayside Evenings

Bayside Promises

Bayside Destinies

Bayside Opposites

Bayside Mistletoe

Bayside Dreams

PARANORMAL ROMANCE

Dark Sea Academy

Mermaid's Song

Mermaid's Heart

Mermaid's Wish

Curse of the Moon

Lost Wolf

Chosen Wolf

Hunted Wolf

Broken Wolf

Cursed Wolf

Secret Jaguar

Valhalla's Curse

Renegade Valkyrie

Pursued Valkyrie

Silenced Valkyrie

Vengeful Valkyrie

Unleashed Valkyrie

The Transformed Series

Deception

Betrayal

Forgotten

Ascension

Duplicity

Sacrifice

Destroyed

Transcend

Entangled

Dauntless

Obscured

Partition

Side Stories:

Fallen

Silent Bite

Hidden Intentions

Saved by a Vampire

Sweet Desire

Paranormal Standalones

Dex

Beauty

Haunted

SHARED WORLD ROMANCES

Indigo Bay Romances

Sweet Dreams

Sweet Reunion

Sweet Complications

Fall into Romance

Lost in Romance

ROMANTIC COMEDIES

(Writing under the pen name Eden Bloom)

Misty Falls Romantic Comedies

Yoga One For Me

All I Want For Christmas is Ewe

Must Love Cats

Happily Ever Laughter

SHORT STORIES

Tiny Bites Collection

COWRITTEN BOOKS

Dead for Good series

Dead for Good

Left for Dead

Dead of Night

Wake the Dead

Dead for Life

AUTHOR'S NOTE

Thank you for reading *Her Last Breath*. I hope you've enjoyed this start to the trilogy. This book has been quite the ride for me, as the author! I started this book and actually got about a third of the way done with the book—that's always an exciting point of the story because it feels like I'm really making progress. But instead of pressing on full steam ahead, I stopped. Not only did I stop, but I set it aside and started working on another book!

A few months later, I had a revelation... It struck me that all of the characters were completely wrong for the story. Not just one or two, but literally ALL of them! I cut two main characters from the storyline, added several new ones, and changed the rest! Not a single character was left as I'd originally cast them.

It was kind of devastating. That's a lot of work out the window. I decided to rewrite the book instead of starting over from scratch. I only ended up with 18% of my original words. But at least I was able to keep that much. As hard as it was to ditch so much work, I'm thrilled about it! Why? Because the new book is SO MUCH better. I'm really excited about this new story, and the new twists and turns are surprising even me!

If you enjoyed this book, please consider leaving a review wherever you purchased it. Not only will your review help me to better understand what you like—so I can give you more of it!—but it will also help other readers find my work. Reviews can be short—just share your honest thoughts. That's it. And they really help—it's like sending chocolate to an author. Seriously!

Want to know when I have a new release? Sign up for new release updates:

http://stacyclaflin.com/newsletter/

I've spent many hours writing, re-writing, and editing this work. I even put together a team who helped with the editing process. As it is impossible to find every single error, if you find any, please contact me through my website and let me know. Then I can fix them for future editions.

Thank you for your support!

~Stacy

LET'S CONNECT

I'd love to connect with you!

Find me on any or all of the following sites. I'm not equally active everywhere, but I'd love to meet you where you love to hang out.

Email: https://stacyclaflin.com/newsletter

I send my newsletter once a week or every other week, and include book updates, new release alerts, freebie notifications, and more. Sometimes I send cat pictures and share interesting facts about my books.

Website: https://stacyclaflin.com/

Find out more about my books on my website. I've written over 80 novels, so chances are, you'll find some books you didn't know about before.

Bookbub: https://www.bookbub.com/authors/stacy-claflin

Bookbub is where I share, rate, and review books that I've

read. You can also get new release and pre-order alerts if you follow me there.

Facebook: https://www.facebook.com/stacy.claflin.author/

Facebook is a huge time suck for me, so I try not to spend too much time there. (I get a lot more writing done that way!) But you can follow me for book updates. I also have a street team you can join: https://www.facebook.com/groups/StacyClaflinStreetTeam/

TikTok: https://www.tiktok.com/@stacyclaflin

TikTok is where I embarrass myself on camera and make videos about my books. I have a lot of fun and share some humorous tips and interesting book/authoring facts.

Pinterest: https://www.pinterest.com/growwithstacy/_saved/

I used to be really active on Pinterest, so there are a lot of fun boards, but I don't update them often. If you like Pinterest, you might enjoy browsing my profile. Just don't expect many updates!

Twitter: https://twitter.com/growwithstacy

Twitter is where I post about book stuff, but I don't interact much.

Instagram: https://www.instagram.com/stacy.claflin/

I'm not super active on Instagram, but I do try to put book updates and pretty pictures when I think about it.

ABOUT THE AUTHOR

Stacy Claflin is a *USA Today* bestselling thriller author who has published more than 100 novels, including Girl in Trouble and The Perfect Death. She has always been curious about the human mind, and in her quest to learn more, she earned a degree in Psychology. Her favorite course was Abnormal Behavior, which has been useful in writing fiction.

Her love for thrillers goes back to her early childhood when she fell in love with Unsolved Mysteries and America's Most Wanted. When Stacy was five, she got mad at a babysitter who wouldn't let her watch the evening news. These days, she spends her free time listening to true crime podcasts or watching documentaries on the subject.

She has been telling stories for as long as she can remember, and as child would often get into trouble for trying to convince friends her wild tales were true. Now she puts her creativity to better use by writing page-turning stories that leave readers begging for more.

Stacy occasionally dabbles in other genres, so as you peruse her library of works, you'll find some romance and paranormal tales, all with strong suspense elements.

For more information:
stacyclaflin.com/about

RESOURCES

Domestic violence and spiritual abuse were both mentioned in this book, and I want to take a moment to acknowledge the seriousness of both issues.

The sad fact is that for too many people one or both of these abuses of power are their lived reality.

If you or someone you know feels controlled, coerced, fearful, threatened, isolated, depressed, anxious, or unsafe in any way—those *could* be signs of experiencing covert abuse.

Abuse is far more than being hit. The legal definitions in many places may surprise you. If someone won't let you leave a room, that is considered abuse in many places. You can call (or possibly text) for help in numerous locations if you are experiencing something like this.

There are many ways to reach out for help if you need it.

You can find safety planning and emergency resources online. Local and national domestic violence advocates are often only a phone call away. There are also therapists and attorneys who specialize in domestic violence care.

<u>Resources:</u>

National Domestic Violence Hotline: 1-800-799-SAFE (7233)
Your local emergency number: 911 or other number.
National Domestic Violence Hotline: https://www.thehotline.org/
Office on Women's Health: https://www.womenshealth.gov/relationships-and-safety/get-help/state-resources

Speak with a professional today for advice, and start planning your safety and exit plans. You deserve to feel safe.

Printed in Great Britain
by Amazon